The Last Tycoon

F. Scott Fitzgerald

ALMA CLASSICS LTD
London House
243-253 Lower Mortlake Road
Richmond
Surrey TW9 2LL
United Kingdom
www.almaclassics.com

The Last Tycoon first published in 1941
This edition first published by Alma Books Ltd in 2013

Extra material © Richard Parker
Notes © Alma Classics Ltd

Cover image: George Barbier

Printed and bound by CPI Group (UK) Ltd, Croydon, CR0 4YY

ISBN: 978-1-84749-318-7

Contents

Other books by F. SCOTT FITZGERALD
published by Alma Classics

All the Sad Young Men

The Beautiful and Damned

The Great Gatsby

Tales of the Jazz Age

Tender Is the Night

This Side of Paradise

F. Scott Fitzgerald (1896–1940)

Edward Fitzgerald,
Fitzgerald's father

Mary McQuillan Fitzgerald,
Fitzgerald's mother

Ginevra King

Zelda Fitzgerald

The Fitzgeralds' house in Montgomery, Alabama

The Fitzgeralds' grave in Rockville, Maryland,
inscribed with the closing line from *The Great Gatsby*

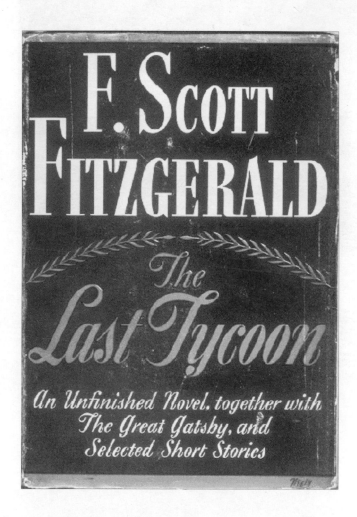

The cover of the first edition of
The Last Tycoon

The Last Tycoon

Chapter 1

T HOUGH I HAVEN'T ever been on the screen I was brought up in pictures. Rudolph Valentino came to my fifth birthday party – or so I was told. I put this down only to indicate that even before the age of reason I was in a position to watch the wheels go round.

I was going to write my memoirs once, *The Producer's Daughter*, but at eighteen you never quite get around to anything like that. It's just as well – it would have been as flat as an old column of Lolly Parsons's.* My father was in the picture business as another man might be in cotton or steel, and I took it tranquilly. At the worst I accepted Hollywood with the resignation of a ghost assigned to a haunted house. I knew what you were supposed to think about it, but I was obstinately unhorrified.

This is easy to say, but harder to make people understand. When I was at Bennington some of the English teachers who pretended an indifference to Hollywood or its products really *hated* it. Hated it way down deep as a threat to their existence. Even before that, when I was in a convent, a sweet little nun asked me to get her a script of a screenplay so she could "teach her class about movie-writing", as she had taught them about the essay and the short story. I got the script for her, and I suppose she puzzled over it and puzzled over it, but it was never mentioned in class, and she gave it back to me with an air of offended surprise and not a single comment. That's what I half-expect to happen to this story.

You can take Hollywood for granted like I did, or you can dismiss it with the contempt we reserve for what we don't understand. It can be understood too, but only dimly and in flashes. Not half a dozen men have ever been able to keep the whole equation of pictures in their heads. And perhaps the closest a woman can come to the set-up is to try and understand one of those men.

The world from an aeroplane I knew. Father always had us travel back and forth that way from school and college. After my sister died when I was a junior, I travelled to and fro alone, and the journey always made me think of her, made me somewhat solemn and subdued. Sometimes there were picture people I knew on board the plane, and occasionally there was an attractive college boy – but not often during the Depression. I seldom really fell asleep during the trip, what with thoughts of Eleanor and the sense of that sharp rip between coast and coast – at least not till we had left those lonely little airports in Tennessee.

This trip was so rough that the passengers divided early into those who turned in right away and those who didn't want to turn in at all. There were two of these latter right across from me, and I was pretty sure from their fragmentary conversation that they were from Hollywood – one of them because he looked like it: a middle-aged Jew, who alternately talked with nervous excitement or else crouched, as if ready to spring, in a harrowing silence; the other a pale, plain, stocky man of thirty, whom I was sure I had seen before. He had been to the house or something. But it might have been when I was a little girl, and so I wasn't offended that he didn't recognize me.

The stewardess – she was tall, handsome and flashing dark, a type that they seemed to run to – asked me if she could make up my berth.

"…and, dear, do you want an aspirin?" She perched on the side of the seat and rocked precariously to and fro with the June hurricane. "…or Nembutal?"

"No."

"I've been so busy with everyone else that I've had no time to ask you." She sat down beside me and buckled us both in. "Do you want some gum?"

This reminded me to get rid of the piece that had been boring me for hours. I wrapped it in a piece of magazine and put it into the automatic ash-holder.

"I can always tell people are nice," the stewardess said approvingly, "if they wrap their gum in paper before they put it in there."

We sat for a while in the half-light of the swaying car. It was vaguely like a swanky restaurant at that twilight time between meals. We were all lingering – and not quite on purpose. Even the stewardess, I think, had to keep reminding herself why she was there.

She and I talked about a young actress I knew, whom she had flown west with two years before. It was in the very lowest time of the Depression, and the young actress kept staring out the window in such an intent way that the stewardess was afraid she was contemplating a leap. It appeared though that she was not afraid of poverty, but only of revolution.

"I know what mother and *I* are going to do," she confided to the stewardess. "We're coming out to the Yellowstone and we're just going to live simply till it all blows over. Then we'll come back. They don't kill artists – you know?"

The proposition pleased me. It conjured up a pretty picture of the actress and her mother being fed by kind Tory* bears who brought them honey, and by gentle fawns who fetched extra milk from the does and then lingered near to make pillows for their heads at night. In turn I told the stewardess about the lawyer and the director who told their plans to Father one night in those brave days. If the bonus army conquered Washington,* the lawyer had a boat hidden in the Sacramento River, and he was going to row upstream for a few months and then come back, "because they always needed lawyers after a revolution to straighten out the legal side".

The director had tended more towards defeatism. He had an old suit, shirt and shoes in waiting – he never did say whether they were his own or whether he got them from the prop department – and he was going to Disappear into the Crowd. I remember Father saying: "But they'll look at your hands! They'll know you haven't done manual work for years. And they'll ask for your union card." And I remember how the director's face fell, and how gloomy he was while he ate his dessert, and how funny and puny they sounded to me.

"Is your father an actor, Miss Brady?" asked the stewardess. "I've certainly heard the name."

At the name Brady, both the men across the aisle looked up. Sideways – that Hollywood look that always seems thrown over one shoulder. Then the young, pale, stocky man unbuttoned his safety strap and stood in the aisle beside us.

"Are you Cecilia *Brady*?" he demanded accusingly, as if I'd been holding out on him. "I *thought* I recognized you. I'm Wylie White."

He could have omitted this – for at the same moment a new voice said, "Watch your step, Wylie!" and another man brushed by him in the aisle and went forward in the direction of the cockpit. Wylie White started and, a little too late, called after him defiantly:

"I only take orders from the pilot."

I recognized the kind of pleasantry that goes on between the powers in Hollywood and their satellites.

The stewardess reproved him:

"Not so loud, please – some of the passengers are asleep."

I saw now that the other man across the aisle, the middle-aged Jew, was on his feet also, staring with shameless economic lechery, after the man who had just gone by. Or rather at the back of the man, who gestured sideways with his hand in a sort of farewell, as he went out of my sight.

I asked the stewardess: "Is he the ass*is*tant pilot?"

She was unbuckling our belt, about to abandon me to Wylie White.

"No. That's Mr Smith. He has the private compartment, the 'bridal suite' – only he has it alone. The assistant pilot is always in uniform." She stood up: "I want to find out if we're going to be grounded in Nashville."

Wylie White was aghast.

"Why?"

"It's a storm coming up in the Mississippi Valley."

"Does that mean we'll have to stay here all *night*?"

"If this keeps up!"

A sudden dip indicated that it would. It tipped Wylie White into the seat opposite me, shunted the stewardess precipitately down in the direction of the cockpit, and plunked the Jewish

7

man into a sitting position. After the studied, unruffled excla-
mations of distaste that befitted the air-minded, we settled
down. There was an introduction.

"Miss Brady – Mr Schwartz," said Wylie White. "He's a
great friend of your father's too."

Mr Schwartz nodded so vehemently that I could almost hear
him saying: "It's true. As God is my judge, it's true!"

He might have said this right out loud at one time in his life
– but he was obviously a man to whom something had happened. Meeting him was like encountering a friend who has
been in a fist fight or collision and got flattened. You stare at
your friend and say: "What happened to you?" And he answers
something unintelligible through broken teeth and swollen lips.
He can't even tell you about it.

Mr Schwartz was physically unmarked; the exaggerated
Persian nose and oblique eyeshadow were as congenital as the
tip-tilted Irish redness around my father's nostrils.

"Nashville!" cried Wylie White. "That means we go to a
hotel. We don't get to the coast till tomorrow night – if then.
My God! I was born in Nashville."

"I should think you'd like to see it again."

"Never – I've kept away for fifteen years. I hope I'll *never*
see it again."

But he would – for the plane was unmistakably going down,
down, down, like Alice in the rabbit hole. Cupping my hand
against the window I saw the blur of the city far away on the
left. The green sign "Fasten your belts – No smoking" had
been on since we first rode into the storm.

"Did you hear what he said?" said Schwartz from one of his
fiery silences across the aisle.

"Hear what?" asked Wylie.

"Hear what he's calling himself," said Schwartz. "Mr *Smith*!"

"Why not?" asked Wylie.

"Oh, nothing," said Schwartz quickly. "I just thought it was funny. Smith." I never heard a laugh with less mirth in it: "Smith!"

I suppose there has been nothing like the airports since the days of the stage stops – nothing quite as lonely, as sombre-silent. The old red-brick depots were built right into the towns they marked – people didn't get off at those isolated stations unless they lived there. But airports lead you way back in history like oases, like the stops on the great trade routes. The sight of air travellers strolling in ones and twos into midnight airports will draw a small crowd any night up to two. The young people look at the planes, the older ones look at the passengers with a watchful incredulity. In the big transcontinental planes we were the coastal rich, who casually alighted from our cloud in mid-America. High adventure might be among us, disguised as a movie star. But mostly it wasn't. And I always wished fervently that we looked more interesting than we did – just as I often have at premieres, when the fans look at you with scornful reproach because you're not a star.

On the ground Wylie and I were suddenly friends, because he held out his arm to steady me when I got out of the plane. From then on, he made a dead set for me – and I didn't mind. From the moment we walked into the airport it had become plain that if we were stranded here we were stranded here together. (It wasn't like the time I lost my boy – the time my boy played the piano with that girl Reina in a little New England farm house near Bennington, and I realized at last I wasn't wanted.

Guy Lombardo* was on the air playing 'Top Hat' and 'Cheek to Cheek',* and she taught him the melodies. The keys falling like leaves and her hands splayed over his as she showed him a black chord. I was a freshman then.)

When we went into the airport Mr Schwartz was along with us too, but he seemed in a sort of dream. All the time we were trying to get accurate information at the desk, he kept staring at the door that led out to the landing field, as if he were afraid the plane would leave without him. Then I excused myself for a few minutes and something happened that I didn't see, but when I came back he and White were standing close together, White talking and Schwartz looking twice as much as if a great truck had just backed up over him. He didn't stare at the door to the landing field any more. I heard the end of Wylie White's remark…

"…I told you to shut up. It serves you right."

"I only said…"

He broke off as I came up and asked if there was any news. It was then half-past two in the morning.

"A little," said Wylie White. "They don't think we'll be able to start for three hours anyhow, so some of the softies are going to a hotel. But I'd like to take you out to the Hermitage, home of Andrew Jackson."*

"How could we see it in the dark?" demanded Schwartz.

"Hell, it'll be sunrise in two hours."

"You two go," said Schwartz.

"All right – you take the bus to the hotel. It's still waiting – *he*'s in there." Wylie's voice had a taunt in it. "Maybe it'd be a good thing."

"No, I'll go along with you," said Schwartz hastily.

We took a taxi in the sudden country dark outside, and he seemed to cheer up. He patted my kneecap encouragingly.

"I should go along," he said, "I should be chaperone. Once upon a time when I was in the big money, I had a daughter – a beautiful daughter."

He spoke as if she had been sold to creditors as a tangible asset.

"You'll have another," Wylie assured him. "You'll get it all back. Another turn of the wheel and you'll be where Cecilia's papa is, won't he, Cecilia?"

"Where is this Hermitage?" asked Schwartz presently. "Far away at the end of nowhere? We will miss the plane?"

"Skip it," said Wylie. "We ought to've brought the stewardess along for you. Didn't you admire the stewardess? *I* thought she was pretty cute."

We drove for a long time over a bright level countryside, just a road and a tree and a shack and a tree, and then suddenly along a winding twist of woodland. I could feel even in the darkness that the trees of the woodland were green – that it was all different from the dusty olive tint of California. Somewhere we passed a Negro driving three cows ahead of him, and they mooed as he scattered them to the side of the road. They were real cows, with warm, fresh, silky flanks, and the Negro grew gradually real out of the darkness, with his big brown eyes staring at us close to the car, as Wylie gave him a quarter. He said, "*Thank* you – thank you," and stood there, and the cows mooed again into the night as we drove off.

I thought of the first sheep I ever remember seeing – hundreds of them, and how our car drove suddenly into them on the back lot of the old Laemmle* studio. They were unhappy about being in pictures, but the men in the car with us kept saying:

"Swell!"

"Is that what you wanted, Dick?"

"Isn't that swell?" And the man named Dick kept standing up in the car as if he were Cortés or Balboa,* looking over that grey fleecy undulation. If I ever knew what picture they were in, I have long forgotten.

We had driven an hour. We crossed a brook over an old rattly iron bridge laid with planks. Now there were roosters crowing and blue-green shadows stirring every time we passed a farmhouse.

"I told you it'd be morning soon," said Wylie. "I was born near here – the son of impoverished southern paupers. The family mansion is now used as an outhouse. We had four servants – my father, my mother and my two sisters. I refused to join the guild, and so I went to Memphis to start my career, which has now reached a dead end." He put his arm around me: "Cecilia, will you marry me, so I can share the Brady fortune?"

He was disarming enough, so I let my head lie on his shoulder.

"What do you do, Cecilia. Go to school?"

"I go to Bennington. I'm a junior."

"Oh, I beg your pardon. I should have known, but I never had the advantage of college training. But a *ju*nior – why I read in *Esquire* that juniors have nothing to learn, Cecilia."

"Why do people think that college girls—"

"Don't apologize – knowledge is power."

"You'd know from the way you talk that we were on our way to Hollywood," I said. "It's always years and years behind the times."

He pretended to be shocked.

"You mean girls in the East have no private lives?"

"That's the point. They *have* got private lives. You're bothering me, let go."

"I can't. It might wake Schwartz, and I think this is the first sleep he's had for weeks. Listen, Cecilia: I once had an affair with the wife of a producer. A very short affair. When it was over she said to me in no uncertain terms, she said: 'Don't you ever tell about this or I'll have you thrown out of Hollywood. My husband's a much more important man than you!'"

I liked him again now, and presently the taxi turned down a long lane fragrant with honeysuckle and narcissus, and stopped beside the great grey hulk of the Andrew Jackson house. The driver turned around to tell us something about it, but Wylie shushed him, pointing at Schwartz, and we tiptoed out of the car.

"You can't get into the Mansion now," the taxi man told us politely.

Wylie and I went and sat against the wide pillars of the steps.

"What about Mr Schwartz?" I asked. "Who is he?"

"To hell with Schwartz. He was the head of some combine once – First National? Paramount? United Artists? Now he's down and out. But he'll be back. You can't flunk out of pictures unless you're a dope or a drunk."

"You don't like Hollywood," I suggested.

"Yes I do. Sure I do. Say! This isn't anything to talk about on the steps of Andrew Jackson's house – at dawn."

"I *like* Hollywood," I persisted.

"It's all right. It's a mining town in lotus land. Who said that? I did. It's a good place for toughies, but I went there from Savannah, Georgia. I went to a garden party the first day. My host shook hands and left me. It was all there – that swimming pool, green moss at two dollars an inch, beautiful felines having drinks and fun…

"…And nobody spoke to me. Not a soul. I spoke to half a dozen people, but they didn't answer. That continued for an hour, two hours – then I got up from where I was sitting and ran out at a dog trot like a crazy man. I didn't feel I had any rightful identity until I got back to the hotel and the clerk handed me a letter addressed to me in my name."

Naturally I hadn't ever had such an experience, but looking back on parties I'd been to, I realized that such things could happen. We don't go for strangers in Hollywood unless they wear a sign saying that their axe has been thoroughly ground elsewhere, and that in any case it's not going to fall on our necks – in other words, unless they're a celebrity. And they'd better look out even then.

"You should have risen above it," I said smugly. "It's not a slam at *you* when people are rude – it's a slam at the people they've met before."

"Such a pretty girl – to say such wise things."

There was an eager to-do in the eastern sky, and Wylie could see me plain – thin with good features and lots of style, and the kicking fetus of a mind. I wonder what I looked like in that dawn, five years ago. A little rumpled and pale, I suppose, but at that age, when one has the young illusion that most adventures are good, I needed only a bath and a change to go on for hours.

Wylie stared at me with really flattering appreciation – and then suddenly we were not alone. Mr Schwartz wandered apologetically into the pretty scene.

"I fell upon a large metal handle," he said, touching the corner of his eye.

Wylie jumped up.

"Just in time, Mr Schwartz," he said. "The tour is just starting. Home of Old Hickory – America's tenth president. The victor of New Orleans, opponent of the National Bank and inventor of the Spoils System."*

Schwartz looked towards me as towards a jury.

"There's a writer for you," he said. "Knows everything and at the same time he knows nothing."

"What's that?" said Wylie, indignant.

It was my first inkling that he was a writer. And while I like writers – because if you ask a writer anything, you usually get an answer – still it belittled him in my eyes. Writers aren't people exactly. Or, if they're any good, they're a whole *lot* of people trying so hard to be one person. It's like actors, who try so pathetically not to look in mirrors, who lean *back*wards trying – only to see their faces in the reflecting chandeliers.

"Ain't writers like that, Cecilia?" demanded Schwartz. "I have no words for them. I only know it's true."

Wylie looked at him with slowly gathering indignation. "I've heard that before," he said. "Look, Manny, I'm a more practical man than you any day! I've sat in an office and listened to some mystic stalk up and down for hours spouting tripe that'd land him on a nut farm anywhere outside of California – and then at the end tell me how *practical* he was, and I was a dreamer – and would I kindly go away and make sense out of what he'd said."

Mr Schwartz's face fell into its more disintegrated alignments. One eye looked upwards through the tall elms. He raised his hand and bit without interest at the cuticle on his second finger. There was a bird flying about the chimney of the house, and his glance followed it. It perched on the chimney pot like a raven, and Mr Schwartz's eyes remained fixed upon it as he said: "We can't get in, and it's time for you two to go back to the plane."

It was still not quite dawn. The Hermitage looked like a nice big white box, but a little lonely and vacated still after a hundred years. We walked back to the car. Only after we had gotten in and Mr Schwartz had surprisingly shut the taxi door on us did we realize he didn't intend to come along.

"I'm not going to the coast – I decided that when I woke up. So I'll stay here, and afterwards the driver could come back for me."

"Going back east?" said Wylie with surprise. "Just because—"

"I have decided," said Schwartz, faintly smiling. "Once I used to be a regular man of decision – you'd be surprised." He felt in his pocket, as the taxi driver warmed up the engine. "Will you give this note to Mr Smith?"

"Shall I come in two hours?" the driver asked Schwartz.

"Yes... sure. I shall be glad to entertain myself looking around."

I kept thinking of him all the way back to the airport – trying to fit him into that early hour and into that landscape. He had come a long way from some ghetto to present himself at that raw shrine. Manny Schwartz and Andrew Jackson – it was hard to say them in the same sentence. It was doubtful if he knew who Andrew Jackson was as he wandered around, but perhaps he figured that if people had preserved his house Andrew Jackson must have been someone who was large and merciful, able to understand. At both ends of life man needed nourishment: a breast – a shrine. Something to lay himself beside when no one wanted him further, and shoot a bullet into his head.

Of course we did not know this for twenty hours. When we got to the airport we told the purser that Mr Schwartz was not continuing, and then forgot about him. The storm had wandered away into eastern Tennessee and broken against the mountains, and we were taking off in less than an hour. Sleepy-eyed travellers appeared from the hotel, and I dozed a few minutes on one of those iron maidens they use for couches. Slowly the idea of a perilous journey was recreated out of the debris of our failure: a new stewardess, tall, handsome, flashing dark, exactly like the other except she wore seersucker instead of French red and blue, went briskly past us with a suitcase. Wylie sat beside me as we waited.

"Did you give the note to Mr Smith?" I asked, half-asleep.

"Yeah."

"Who is Mr Smith? I suspect he spoilt Mr Schwartz's trip."

"It was Schwartz's fault."

"I'm prejudiced against steamrollers," I said. "My father tries to be a steamroller around the house, and I tell him to save it for the studio."

I wondered if I was being fair; words are the palest counters at that time in the morning. "Still, he steamrollered me into Bennington and I've always been grateful for that."

"There would be quite a crash," Wylie said, "if Steamroller Brady met Steamroller Smith."

"Is Mr Smith a competitor of Father's?"

"Not exactly. I should say no. But if he was a competitor I know where my money would be."

"On Father?"

"I'm afraid not."

It was too early in the morning for family patriotism. The pilot was at the desk with the purser and he shook his head as they regarded a prospective passenger who had put two nickels in the electric phonograph and lay alcoholically on a bench fighting off sleep. The first song he had chosen, 'Lost', thundered through the room, followed, after a slight interval, by his other choice, 'Gone',* which was equally dogmatic and final. The pilot shook his head emphatically and walked over to the passenger.

"Afraid we're not going to be able to carry you this time, old man."

"Wha'?"

The drunk sat up, awful-looking, yet discernibly attractive, and I was sorry for him in spite of his passionately ill-chosen music.

"Go back to the hotel and get some sleep. There'll be another plane tonight."

"Only going up in ee *air*."

"Not this time, old man."

In his disappointment the drunk fell off the bench – and above the phonograph, a loudspeaker summoned us respectable people outside. In the corridor of the plane I ran into Monroe Stahr and fell all over him, or wanted to. There was a man any girl would go for, with or without encouragement. I was emphatically with*out* it, but he liked me and sat down opposite till the plane took off.

"Let's all ask for our money back," he suggested. His dark eyes took me in, and I wondered what they would look like if he fell in love. They were kind, aloof and, though they often reasoned with you gently, somewhat superior. It was no fault of theirs if they saw so much. He darted in and out of the role of "one of the boys" with dexterity – but on the whole I should say he wasn't one of them. But he knew how to shut up, how to draw into the background, how to listen. From where he stood (and though he was not a tall man, it always seemed high up) he watched the multitudinous practicalities of his world like a proud young shepherd to whom night and day had never mattered. He was born sleepless, without a talent for rest or the desire for it.

We sat in unembarrassed silence – I had known him since he became Father's partner a dozen years ago, when I was seven and Stahr was twenty-two. Wylie was across the aisle and I didn't know whether or not to introduce them, but Stahr kept turning his ring so abstractedly that he made me feel young and invisible, and I didn't care. I never dared look quite away from him or quite *at* him, unless I had something important to say – and I knew he affected many other people in the same manner.

"I'll *give* you this ring, Cecilia."

"I beg your pardon. I didn't realize that I was—"

"I've got half a dozen like it."

He handed it to me, a gold nugget with the letter S in bold relief. I had been thinking how oddly its bulk contrasted with his fingers, which were delicate and slender like the rest of his body, and like his slender face with the arched eyebrows and the dark curly hair. He looked spiritual at times, but he was a fighter – somebody out of his past knew him when he was one of a gang of kids in the Bronx, and gave me a description of how he walked always at the head of his gang, this rather frail boy, occasionally throwing a command backwards out of the corner of his mouth.

Stahr folded my hand over the ring, stood up and addressed Wylie.

"Come up to the bridal suite," he said. "See you later, Cecilia."

Before they went out of hearing, I heard Wylie's question: "Did you open Schwartz's note?" And Stahr:

"Not yet."

I must be slow, for only then did I realize that Stahr was Mr Smith.

Afterwards Wylie told me what was in the note. Written by the headlights of the taxi, it was almost illegible.

Dear Monroe,

You are the best of them all I have always admired your mentality so when you turn against me I know it's no use! I must be no good and am not going to continue the journey let me warn you once again look out! I know.

Your friend

Manny

Stahr read it twice, and raised his hand to the morning stubble on his chin.

"He's a nervous wreck," he said. "There's nothing to be done – absolutely nothing. I'm sorry I was short with him – but I don't like a man to approach me telling me it's for *my* sake."

"Maybe it was," said Wylie.

"It's poor technique."

"I'd fall for it," said Wylie. "I'm vain as a woman. If anybody pretends to be interested in me, I'll ask for more. I like advice."

Stahr shook his head distastefully. Wylie kept on ribbing him – he was one of those to whom this privilege was permitted.

"You fall for some kinds of flattery," he said. "This 'little Napoleon stuff'."

"It makes me sick," said Stahr, "but it's not as bad as some man trying to help you."

"If you don't like advice, why do you pay *me*?"

"That's a question of merchandise," said Stahr. "I'm a merchant. I want to buy what's in your mind."

"You're no merchant," said Wylie. "I knew a lot of them when I was a publicity man, and I agree with Charles Francis Adams."*

"What did he say?"

"He knew them all – Gould, Vanderbilt, Carnegie, Astor* – and he said there wasn't one he'd care to meet again in the hereafter. Well – they haven't improved since then, and that's why I say you're no merchant."

"Adams was probably a sourbelly," said Stahr. "He wanted to be head man himself, but he didn't have the judgement or else the character."

"He had brains," said Wylie rather tartly.

"It takes more than brains. You writers and artists poop out and get all mixed up, and somebody has to come in and straighten you out." He shrugged his shoulders. "You seem to take things so personally, hating people and worshipping them – always thinking people are so important – especially yourselves. You just ask to be kicked around. I like people and I like them to like me, but I wear my heart where God put it – on the inside."

He broke off.

"What did I say to Schwartz in the airport? Do you remember – exactly?"

"You said, 'Whatever you're after, the answer is No!'" Stahr was silent.

"He was sunk," said Wylie, "but I laughed him out of it. We took Billy Brady's daughter for a ride."

Stahr rang for the stewardess.

"That pilot," he said, "would he mind if I sat up in front with him a while?"

"That's against the rules, Mr Smith."

"Ask him to step in here a minute when he's free."

Stahr sat up front all afternoon. While we slid off the endless desert and over the tablelands, dyed with many colours like the white sands we dyed with colours when I was a child. Then in the late afternoon, the peaks themselves – the Mountains of the Frozen Saw – slid under our propellers and we were close to home.

When I wasn't dozing I was thinking that I wanted to marry Stahr, that I wanted to make him love me. Oh, the conceit! What on earth did I have to offer? But I didn't think like that then. I had the pride of young women, which draws its strength from such sublime thoughts as: "I'm as good as *she* is." For my purposes I was just as beautiful as the great beauties who must have inevitably thrown themselves at his head. My little spurt of intellectual interest was of course making me fit to be a brilliant ornament of any salon.

I know now it was absurd. Though Stahr's education was founded on nothing more than a night-school course in stenography, he had a long time ago run ahead through trackless wastes of perception into fields where very few men were able to follow him. But in my reckless conceit I matched my grey eyes against his brown ones for guile, my young golf-and-tennis heartbeats against his, which must be slowing a little after years of overwork. And I planned and I contrived and I plotted – any women can tell you – but it never came to anything, as you will see. I still like to think that if he'd been a poor boy and nearer my age I could have managed it, but of course the real truth was that I had nothing to offer that he didn't have; some of my more romantic ideas actually stemmed from pictures – *42nd Street*,* for example, had a great influence on me. It's more than possible that some of the pictures which Stahr himself conceived had shaped me into what I was.

So it was rather hopeless. Emotionally, at least, people can't live by taking in each other's washing.

But at that time it was different: Father might help, the stewardess might help. She might go up in the cockpit and say to Stahr: "If I ever saw love, it's in that girl's eyes."

The pilot might help: "Man, are you blind? Why don't you go back there?"

Wylie White might help – instead of standing in the aisle looking at me doubtfully, wondering whether I was awake or asleep.

"Sit down," I said. "What's new? Where are we?"

"Up in the air."

"Oh, so that's it. Sit down." I tried to show a cheerful interest: "What are you writing?"

"Heaven help me, I am writing about a boy scout – *the* boy scout."

"Is it Stahr's idea?"

"I don't know – he told me to look into it. He may have ten writers working ahead of me or behind me, a system which he so thoughtfully invented. So you're in love with him?"

"I should say not," I said indignantly. "I've known him all my life."

"Desperate, eh? Well, I'll arrange it if you'll use all your influence to advance me. I want a unit of my own." .

I closed my eyes and drifted off. When I woke up, the stewardess was putting a blanket over me.

"Almost there," she said.

Out the window I could see by the sunset that we were in a greener land.

"I just heard something funny," she volunteered, "up in the cockpit – that Mr Smith – or Mr Stahr – I never remember seeing his name—"

"It's never on any pictures," I said.

"Oh. Well, he's been asking the pilots a lot about flying – I mean, he's interested? You *know*?"

"I know."

"I mean one of them told me he bet he could teach Mr Stahr solo flying in ten minutes. He has such a fine mentality, that's what he said."

I was getting impatient.

"Well, what was so funny?"

"Well, finally one of the pilots asked Mr Smith if he liked his business, and Mr Smith said, 'Sure. Sure I like it. It's nice being the only sound nut in a hatful of cracked ones.'"

The stewardess doubled up with laughter – and I could have spit at her.

"I mean calling all those people a hatful of nuts. I mean *cracked* nuts." Her laughter stopped with unexpected suddenness, and her face was grave as she stood up. "Well, I've got to finish my chart."

"Goodbye."

Obviously Stahr had put the pilots right up on the throne with him and let them rule with him for a while. Years later I travelled with one of those same pilots and he told me one thing Stahr had said.

He was looking down at the mountains.

"Suppose you were a railroad man," he said. "You have to send a train through there somewhere. Well, you get your surveyors' reports, and you find there's three or four or half a dozen gaps, and not one is better than the other. You've got to decide – on what basis? You can't test the best way – except by doing it. So you just do it."

The pilot thought he had missed something.

"How do you mean?"

"You choose some one way for no reason at all – because that mountain's pink or the blueprint is a better blue. You see?"

The pilot considered that this was very valuable advice. But he doubted if he'd ever be in a position to apply it.

"What I wanted to know," he told me ruefully, "is how he ever got to be Mr Stahr."

I'm afraid Stahr could never have answered that one, for the embryo is not equipped with a memory. But I could answer a little. He had flown up very high to see, on strong wings, when he was young. And while he was up there he had looked on all the kingdoms,* with the kind of eyes that can stare straight into the sun. Beating his wings tenaciously – finally frantically – and keeping on beating them, he had stayed up there longer than most of us, and then, remembering all he had seen from his great height of how things were, he had settled gradually to earth.

The motors were off, and all our five senses began to readjust themselves for landing. I could see a line of lights for the Long Beach Naval Station ahead and to the left, and on the right a twinkling blur for Santa Monica. The California moon was out, huge and orange over the Pacific. However I happened to feel about these things – and they were home, after all – I know that Stahr must have felt much more. These were the things I had first opened my eyes on, like the sheep on the back lot of the old Laemmle studio; but this was where Stahr had come to earth after that extraordinary illuminating flight where he saw which way we were going, and how we looked doing it, and how much of it mattered. You could say that this was where an accidental wind blew him, but I don't think so. I would rather think that in a "long shot" he saw a new way of measuring our jerky hopes and graceful rogueries and awkward sorrows, and that he came here from choice to be with us to the end. Like the plane coming down into the Glendale airport, into the warm darkness.

Chapter 2

I T WAS NINE O'CLOCK of a July night and there were still some extras in the drugstore across from the studio – I could see them bent over the pin games inside – as I parked my car. "Old" Johnny Swanson stood on the corner in his semi-cowboy clothes, staring gloomily past the moon. Once he had been as big in pictures as Tom Mix or Bill Hart* – now it was too sad to speak to him, and I hurried across the street and through the front gate.

There is never a time when a studio is absolutely quiet. There is always a night shift of technicians in the laboratories and dubbing rooms and people on the maintenance staff dropping in at the commissary. But the sounds are all different – the padded hush of tyres, the quiet tick of a motor running idle, the naked cry of a soprano singing into a night-bound microphone. Around a corner I came upon a man in rubber boots washing down a car in a wonderful white light – a fountain among the dead industrial shadows. I slowed up as I saw Mr Marcus being hoisted into his car in front of the administration building, because he took so long to say anything, even goodnight – and while I waited I realized that the soprano was singing, "Come, come, I love you only"* over and over; I remember this because she kept singing the same line during the earthquake. That didn't come for five minutes yet.

Father's offices were in the old building with the long balconies and iron rails with their suggestion of a perpetual tightrope. Father was on the second floor, with Stahr on one side and Mr Marcus on the other – this evening there were lights all along the row. My stomach dipped a little at the proximity to Stahr, but that was in pretty good control now – I'd seen him only once in the month I'd been home.

There were a lot of strange things about Father's office, but I'll make it brief. In the outer part were three poker-faced secretaries who had sat there like witches ever since I could remember – Birdy Peters, Maude something and Rosemary Schmiel; I don't know whether this was her name, but she was the dean of the trio, so to speak, and under her desk was the kick lock that admitted you to Father's throne room. All three of the secretaries were passionate capitalists, and Birdy had invented the rule that if typists were seen eating together more than once in a single week they were hauled up on the carpet. At that time the studios feared mob rule.

I went on in. Nowadays all chief executives have huge drawing rooms, but my father's was the first. It was also the first to have one-way glass in the big French windows, and I've heard a story about a trap in the floor that would drop unpleasant visitors to an oubliette below, but believe it to be an invention. There was a big painting of Will Rogers, hung conspicuously and intended, I think, to suggest Father's essential kinship with Hollywood's St Francis;* there was a signed photograph of Minna Davis, Stahr's dead wife, and photos of other studio celebrities and big chalk drawings of Mother and me. Tonight the one-way French windows were open and a big moon, rosy gold with a haze around, was wedged helpless in one of them.

Father and Jacques La Borwitz and Rosemary Schmiel were down at the end around a big circular desk.

What did Father look like? I couldn't describe him except for once in New York when I met him where I didn't expect to; I was aware of a bulky, middle-aged man who looked a little ashamed of himself, and I wished he'd move on – and then I saw he was Father. Afterwards I was shocked at my impression. Father can be very magnetic – he had a tough jaw and an Irish smile.

But as for Jacques La Borwitz, I shall spare you. Let me just say he was an assistant producer, which is something like a commissar, and let it go at that. Where Stahr picked up such mental cadavers or had them forced upon him – or especially how he got any use out of them – has always amazed me, as it amazed everyone fresh from the East who slapped up against them. Jacques La Borwitz had his points, no doubt, but so have the sub-microscopic protozoa, so has a dog prowling for a bitch and a bone. Jacques La – oh my!

From their expressions I was sure they had been talking about Stahr. Stahr had ordered something or forbidden something, or defied Father or junked one of La Borwitz's pictures or something catastrophic, and they were sitting there in protest at night in a community of rebellion and helplessness. Rosemary Schmiel sat pad in hand, as if ready to write down their dejection.

"I'm to drive you home dead or alive," I told Father. "All those birthday presents rotting away in their packages!"

"A birthday!" cried Jacques in a flurry of apology. "How old? I didn't know."

"Forty-three," said Father distinctly.

He was older than that – four years – and Jacques knew it; I saw him note it down in his account book to use sometime. Out here these account books are carried open in the hand. One can see the entries being made without recourse to lip-reading, and Rosemary Schmiel was compelled in emulation to make a mark on her pad. As she rubbed it out, the earth quaked under us.

We didn't get the full shock like at Long Beach, where the upper storeys of shops were spewed into the streets and small hotels drifted out to sea – but for a full minute our bowels were one with the bowels of the earth – like some nightmare attempt to attach our navel cords again and jerk us back to the womb of creation.

Mother's picture fell off the wall, revealing a small safe – Rosemary and I grabbed frantically for each other and did a strange screaming waltz across the room. Jacques fainted, or at least disappeared, and Father clung to his desk and shouted, "Are you all right?" Outside the window the singer came to the climax of "I love you only", held it a moment and then, I swear, started it all over. Or maybe they were playing it back to her from the recording machine.

The room stood still, shimmying a little. We made our way to the door, suddenly including Jacques, who had reappeared, and tottered out dizzily through the anteroom onto the iron balcony. Almost all the lights were out, and from here and there we could hear cries and calls. Momentarily we stood waiting for a second shock – then, as with a common impulse, we went into Stahr's entry and through to his office.

The office was big, but not as big as Father's. Stahr sat on the side of his couch rubbing his eyes. When the quake came he had been asleep, and he wasn't sure yet whether he had dreamt it. When we convinced him he thought it was all rather funny – until the telephones began to ring. I watched him as unobtrusively as possible. He was grey with fatigue while he listened to the phone and dictagraph, but as the reports came in, his eyes began to pick up shine.

"A couple of water mains have burst," he said to Father. "They're heading into the back lot."

"Gray's shooting in the French Village," said Father.

"It's flooded around the Station too, and in the Jungle and the City Corner. What the hell – nobody seems to be hurt." In passing, he shook my hands gravely: "Where've you been, Cecilia?"

"You going out there, Monroe?" Father asked.

"When all the news is in: one of the power lines is off too – I've sent for Robinson."

He made me sit down with him on the couch and tell about the quake again.

"You look tired," I said, cute and motherly.

"Yes," he agreed. "I've got no place to go in the evenings, so I just work."

"I'll arrange some evenings for you."

"I used to play poker with a gang," he said thoughtfully, "before I was married. But they all drank themselves to death."

Miss Doolan, his secretary, came in with fresh bad news.

"Robby'll take care of everything when he comes," Stahr assured Father. He turned to me. "Now there's a man – that Robinson. He was a troubleshooter – fixed the telephone wires in Minnesota blizzards – nothing stumps him. He'll be here in a minute – you'll like Robby."

He said it as if it had been his lifelong intention to bring us together, and he had arranged the whole earthquake with just that in mind.

"Yes, you'll like Robby," he repeated. "When do you go back to college?"

"I've just come home."

"You get the whole summer?"

"I'm sorry," I said. "I'll go back as soon as I can."

I was in a mist. It hadn't failed to cross my mind that he might have some intention about me, but if it was so, it was in an exasperatingly early stage – I was merely "a good property". And the idea didn't seem so attractive at that moment – like marrying a doctor. He seldom left the studio before eleven.

"How long," he asked my father, "before she graduates from college? That's what I was trying to say."

And I think I was about to sing out eagerly that I needn't go back at all, that I was quite educated already – when the totally admirable Robinson came in. He was a bow-legged young redhead, all ready to go.

"This is Robby, Cecilia," said Stahr. "Come on, Robby."

So I met Robby. I can't say it seemed like fate – but it was. For it was Robby who later told me how Stahr found his love that night.

* * *

Under the moon the back lot was thirty acres of fairyland – not because the locations really looked like African jungles and French chateaux and schooners at anchor and Broadway at night, but because they looked like the torn picture books of childhood, like fragments of stories dancing in an open fire. I never lived in a house with an attic, but a back lot must be something like that, and at night of course, in an enchanted distorted way, it all comes true.

When Stahr and Robby arrived, clusters of lights had already picked out the danger spots in the flood.

"We'll pump it out into the swamp on Thirty-Sixth Street," said Robby after a moment. "It's city property – but isn't this an act of God? Say – look there!"

On top of a huge head of the Goddess Shiva, two women were floating down the current of an impromptu river. The idol had come unloosed from a set of Burma, and it meandered earnestly on its way, stopping sometimes to waddle and bump in the shallows with the other debris of the tide. The two refugees had found sanctuary along a scroll of curls on its bald forehead and seemed at first glance to be sightseers on an interesting bus ride through the scene of the flood.

"Will you look at that, Monroe!" said Robby. "Look at those dames!"

Dragging their legs through sudden bogs, they made their way to the bank of the stream. Now they could see the women, looking a little scared but brightening at the prospect of rescue.

"We ought to let 'em drift out to the waste pipe," said Robby gallantly, "but DeMille* needs that head next week."

He wouldn't have hurt a fly, though, and presently he was hip-deep in the water, fishing for them with a pole and succeeding only in spinning it in a dizzy circle. Help arrived, and the impression quickly got around that one of them was very pretty, and then that they were people of importance. But they were just strays, and Robby waited disgustedly to give them hell while the thing was brought finally into control and beached.

"Put that head back!" he called up to them. "You think it's a souvenir?"

One of the women came sliding smoothly down the cheek of the idol, and Robby caught her and set her on solid ground; the other one hesitated and then followed. Robby turned to Stahr for judgement.

"What'll we do with them, chief?"

Stahr did not answer. Smiling faintly at him from not four feet away was the face of his dead wife, identical even to the expression. Across the four feet of moonlight, the eyes he knew looked back at him, a curl blew a little on a familiar forehead; the smile lingered, changed a little according to pattern; the lips parted – the same. An awful fear went over him, and he wanted to cry aloud. Back from the still-sour room, the muffled glide of the limousine hearse, the falling concealing flowers, from out there in the dark – here now warm and glowing. The river passed him in a rush, the great spotlights swooped and blinked – and then he heard another voice speak that was not Minna's voice.

"We're sorry," said the voice. "We followed a truck in through a gate."

A little crowd had gathered – electricians, grips, truckers – and Robby began to nip at them like a sheepdog.

"...get the big pumps on the tanks on Stage 4... put a cable around this head... raft it up on a couple of two-by-fours... get the water out of the jungle first, for Christ's sake... that big 'A' pipe, lay it down... all that stuff is plastic...."

Stahr stood watching the two women as they threaded their way after a policeman towards an exit gate. Then he took a tentative step to see if the weakness had gone out of his knees. A loud tractor came bumping through the slush, and men began streaming by him – every second one glancing at him, smiling, speaking: "Hello, Monroe… Hello, Mr Stahr… wet night, Mr Stahr… Monroe… Monroe… Stahr… Stahr… Stahr."

He spoke and waved back as the people streamed by in the darkness, looking, I suppose, a little like the Emperor and the Old Guard.* There is no world so but it has its heroes, and Stahr was the hero. Most of these men had been here a long time – through the beginnings and the great upset, when sound came, and the three years of depression, he had seen that no harm came to them. The old loyalties were trembling now, there were clay feet everywhere, but still he was their man, the last of the princes. And their greeting was a sort of low cheer as they went by.

Chapter 3

B ETWEEN THE NIGHT I GOT BACK and the quake, I'd
made many observations.

About Father, for example. I loved Father – in a sort of
irregular graph with many low swoops – but I began to see
that his strong will didn't fill him out as a passable man.
Most of what he accomplished boiled down to shrewd. He
had acquired with luck and shrewdness a quarter-interest in
a booming circus – together with young Stahr. That was his
life's effort – all the rest was an instinct to hang on. Of course,
he talked that double talk to Wall Street about how mysterious
it was to make a picture, but Father didn't know the ABCs of
dubbing or even cutting. Nor had he learnt much about the
feel of America as a bar boy in Ballyhegan, nor did he have
any more than a drummer's sense of a story. On the other
hand, he didn't have concealed paresis like —; he came to the
studio before noon and, with a suspiciousness developed like
a muscle, it was hard to put anything over on him.

Stahr had been his luck – and Stahr was something else
again. He was a marker in industry like Edison and Lumière
and Griffith* and Chaplin. He led pictures way up past the
range and power of the theatre, reaching a sort of golden age
before the censorship.

Proof of his leadership was the spying that went on around
him – not just for inside information or patented process

36

secrets – but spying on his scent for a trend in taste, his guess as to how things were going to be. Too much of his vitality was taken by the mere parrying of these attempts. It made his work secret in part, often devious, slow – and hard to describe as the plans of a general, where the psychological factors become too tenuous and we end by merely adding up the successes and failures. But I have determined to give you a glimpse of him functioning, which is my excuse for what follows. It is drawn partly from a paper I wrote in college on 'A Producer's Day' and partly from my imagination. More often I have blocked in the ordinary events myself, while the stranger ones are true.

* * *

In the early morning after the flood, a man walked up to the outside balcony of the Administration Building. He lingered there some time, according to an eyewitness, then mounted to the iron railing and dove head first to the pavement below. Breakage – one arm.

Miss Doolan, Stahr's secretary, told him about it when he buzzed for her at nine. He had slept in his office without hearing the small commotion.

"Pete Zavras!…" Stahr exclaimed. "The camera man?"

"They took him to a doctor's office. It won't be in the paper."

"Hell of a thing," he said. "I knew he'd gone to pot – but I don't know why. He was all right when we used him two years ago – why should he come here? How did he get in?"

"He bluffed it with his old studio pass," said Catherine Doolan. She was a dry hawk, the wife of an assistant director. "Perhaps the quake had something to do with it."

"He was the best camera man in town," Stahr said. When he had heard of the hundreds dead at Long Beach, he was still haunted by the abortive suicide at dawn. He told Catherine Doolan to trace the matter down.

The first dictagraph messages blew in through the warm morning. While he shaved and had coffee, he talked and listened. Robby had left a message: "If Mr Stahr wants me, tell him: to hell with it, I'm in bed." An actor was sick or thought so; the Governor of California was bringing a party out; a supervisor had beaten up his wife for the prints and must be "reduced to a writer" – these three affairs were Father's job – unless the actor was under personal contract to Stahr. There was early snow on a location in Canada with the company already there – Stahr raced over the possibilities of salvage, reviewing the story of the picture. Nothing. Stahr called Catherine Doolan.

"I want to speak to the cop who put two women off the back lot last night. I think his name's Malone."

"Yes, Mr Stahr. I've got Joe Wyman – about the trousers."

"Hello, Joe," said Stahr. "Listen – two people at the sneak preview complained that Morgan's* fly was open for half the picture... of course they're exaggerating, but even if it's only ten feet... no, we can't find the people, but I want that picture run over and over until you find that footage. Get a lot of people in the projection room – somebody'll spot it."

"Tout passe. – L'art robuste
*Seul a l'éternité."**

"And there's the Prince from Denmark,"* said Catherine Doolan. "He's very handsome." She was impelled to add pointlessly: "...for a tall man."

"Thanks," Stahr said. "Thank you, Catherine, I appreciate it that I am now the handsomest small man on the lot. Send the Prince out on the sets and tell him we'll lunch at one."

"And Mr George Boxley – looking very angry in a British way."

"I'll see him for ten minutes."

As she went out, he asked: "Did Robby phone in?"

"No."

"Call sound, and if he's been heard from, call him and ask him this. Ask him this: did he hear that woman's name last night? Either of those women. Or anything so they could be traced."

"Anything else?"

"No, but tell him it's important while he still remembers. What were they? I mean what kind of people – ask him that too. I mean were they..."

She waited, scratching his words on her pad without looking.

"...oh, were they... questionable? Were they theatrical? Never mind – skip that. Just ask if he knows how they can be traced."

The policeman, Malone, had known nothing. Two dames, and he had hustled 'em, you betcha. One of them was sore. Which one? One of them. They had a car, a Chevy – he thought of taking the licence. Was it – the good looker who was sore? It was one of them.

Not which one – he had noticed nothing. Even on the lot here Minna was forgotten. In three years. So much for that then.

Stahr smiled at Mr George Boxley. It was a kindly fatherly smile Stahr had developed inversely when he was a young man pushed into high places. Originally it had been a smile of respect towards his elders; then, as his own decisions grew rapidly to displace theirs, a smile so that they should not feel it; finally emerging as what it was: a smile of kindness – sometimes a little hurried and tired, but always there – towards anyone who had not angered him within the hour. Or anyone he did not intend to insult, aggressive and outright.

Mr Boxley did not smile back. He came in with the air of being violently dragged, though no one apparently had a hand on him. He stood in front of a chair, and again it was as if two invisible attendants seized his arms and set him down forcibly into it. He sat there morosely. Even when he lit a cigarette on Stahr's invitation, one felt that the match was held to it by exterior forces he disdained to control.

Stahr looked at him courteously.

"Something not going well, Mr Boxley?"

The novelist looked back at him in thunderous silence.

"I read your letter," said Stahr. The tone of the pleasant young headmaster was gone. He spoke as to an equal, with a faint two-edged deference.

"I can't get what I write on paper," broke out Boxley. "You've all been very decent, but it's a sort of conspiracy. Those two hacks you've teamed me with listen to what I say, but they spoil it – they seem to have a vocabulary of about a hundred words."

"Why don't you write it yourself?" asked Stahr.

"I have. I sent you some."

"But it was just talk, back and forth," said Stahr mildly. "Interesting talk but nothing more."

Now it was all the two ghostly attendants could do to hold Boxley in the deep chair. He struggled to get up; he uttered a single quiet bark which had some relation to laughter but none to amusement, and said:

"I don't think you people read things. The men are duelling when the conversation takes place. At the end one of them falls into a well and has to be hauled up in a bucket."

He barked again and subsided.

"Would you write that in a book of your own, Mr Boxley?"

"What? Naturally not."

"You'd consider it too cheap."

"Movie standards are different," said Boxley, hedging.

"Do you ever go to them?"

"No – almost never."

"Isn't it because people are always duelling and falling down wells?"

"Yes – and wearing strained facial expressions and talking incredible and unnatural dialogue."

"Skip the dialogue for a minute," said Stahr. "Granted your dialogue is more graceful than what these hacks can write – that's why we brought you out here. But let's imagine something that isn't either bad dialogue or jumping down a well. Has your office got a stove in it that lights with a match?"

"I think it has," said Boxley stiffly, "but I never use it."

"Suppose you're in your office. You've been fighting duels or writing all day and you're too tired to fight or write any more. You're sitting there staring – dull, like we all get sometimes. A pretty stenographer that you've seen before comes into the room and you watch her – idly. She doesn't see you, though you're very close to her. She takes off her gloves, opens her purse and dumps it out on a table..."

Stahr stood up, tossing his keyring on his desk.

"She has two dimes and a nickel – and a cardboard match box. She leaves the nickel on the desk, puts the two dimes back into her purse and takes her black gloves to the stove, opens it and puts them inside. There is one match in the matchbox and she starts to light it kneeling by the stove. You notice that there's a stiff wind blowing in the window – but just then your telephone rings. The girl picks it up, says hello – listens – and says deliberately into the phone, 'I've never owned a pair of black gloves in my life.' She hangs up, kneels by the stove again and, just as she lights the match, you glance around very suddenly and see that there's another man in the office, watching every move the girl makes…"

Stahr paused. He picked up his keys and put them in his pocket.

"Go on," said Boxley, smiling. "What happens?"

"I don't know," said Stahr. "I was just making pictures."

Boxley felt he was being put in the wrong.

"It's just melodrama," he said.

"Not necessarily," said Stahr. "In any case, nobody has moved violently or talked cheap dialogue or had any facial expression at all. There was only one bad line, and a writer like you could improve it. But you were interested."

"What was the nickel for?" asked Boxley evasively.

"I don't know," said Stahr. Suddenly he laughed. "Oh, yes – the nickel was for the movies."

The two invisible attendants seemed to release Boxley. He relaxed, leant back in his chair and laughed.

"What in hell do you pay me for?" he demanded. "I don't understand the damn stuff."

"You will," said Stahr grinning, "or you wouldn't have asked about the nickel."

* * *

A dark, saucer-eyed man was waiting in the outer office as they came out.

"Mr Boxley, this is Mr Mike Van Dyke," Stahr said. "What is it, Mike?"

"Nothing," Mike said. "I just came up to see if you were real."

"Why don't you go to work?" Stahr said. "I haven't had a laugh in the rushes for days."

"I'm afraid of a nervous breakdown."

"You ought to keep in form," Stahr said. "Let's see you peddle your stuff." He turned to Boxley: "Mike's a gag man – he was out here when I was in the cradle. Mike, show Mr Boxley a double wing, clutch, kick and scram."

"Here?" asked Mike.

"Here."

"There isn't much room. I wanted to ask you about—"

"There's lots of room."

"Well," he looked around tentatively. "You shoot the gun."

Miss Doolan's assistant, Katy, took a paper bag, blew it open.

"It was a routine," Mike said to Boxley, "back in the Keystone days." He turned to Stahr: "Does he know what a routine is?"

"It means an act," Stahr explained. "Georgie Jessel* talks about 'Lincoln's Gettysburg routine'."

Katy poised the neck of the blown-up bag in her mouth. Mike stood with his back to her.

"Ready?" Katy asked. She brought her hands down on the side. Immediately Mike grabbed his bottom with both hands, jumped in the air, slid his feet out on the floor one after the

43

other, remaining in place and flapping his arms twice like a bird –

"Double wing," said Stahr.

– and then ran out the screen door which the office boy held open for him and disappeared past the window of the balcony.

"Mr Stahr," said Miss Doolan, "Mr Hanson is on the phone from New York."

Ten minutes later he clicked his dictagraph, and Miss Doolan came in. There was a male star waiting to see him in the outer office, Miss Doolan said.

"Tell him I went out by the balcony," Stahr advised her.

"All right. He's been in four times this week. He seems very anxious."

"Did he give you any hint of what he wanted? Isn't it something he can see Mr Brady about?"

"He didn't say. You have a conference coming up. Miss Meloney and Mr White are outside. Mr Broaca is next door in Mr Reinmund's office."

"Send Mr Roderiguez in," said Stahr. "Tell him I can see him only for a minute."

When the handsome actor came in, Stahr remained standing.

"What is it that can't wait?" he asked pleasantly.

The actor waited carefully till Miss Doolan had gone out.

"Monroe, I'm through," he said. "I had to see you."

"Through!" said Stahr. "Have you seen *Variety*? Your picture's held over at Roxy's and did thirty-seven thousand in Chicago last week."

"That's the worst of it. That's the tragedy. I get everything I want, and now it means nothing."

"Well, go on, explain."

"There's nothing between Esther and me any more. There never can be again."

"A row."

"Oh, no – worse – I can't bear to mention it. My head's in a daze. I wander around like a madman. I go through my part as if I was asleep."

"I haven't noticed it," said Stahr. "You were great in your rushes yesterday."

"Was I? That just shows you nobody ever guesses."

"Are you trying to tell me that you and Esther are separating?"

"I suppose it'll come to that. Yes – inevitably – it will."

"What was it?" demanded Stahr impatiently. "Did she come in without knocking?"

"Oh, there's nobody else. It's just… me. I'm through."

Stahr got it suddenly.

"How do you know?"

"It's been true for six weeks."

"It's your imagination," said Stahr. "Have you been to a doctor?"

The actor nodded.

"I've tried everything. I even… one day in desperation I went down to… to Claris. But it was hopeless. I'm washed up."

Stahr had an impish temptation to tell him to go to Brady about it. Brady handled all matters of public relations. Or was this private relations. He turned away for a moment, got his face in control, turned back.

"I've been to Pat Brady," said the star, as if guessing the thought. "He gave me a lot of phoney advice and I tried it all, but nothing doing. Esther and I sit opposite each other at

dinner, and I'm ashamed to look at her. She's been a good sport
about it, but I'm ashamed. I'm ashamed all day long. I think
Rainy Day grossed twenty-five thousand in Des Moines and
broke all records in St Louis and did twenty-seven thousand
in Kansas City. My fan mail's way up, and there I am afraid
to go home at night, afraid to go to bed."

Stahr began to be faintly oppressed. When the actor first
came in, Stahr had intended to invite him to a cocktail party,
but now it scarcely seemed appropriate. What would he want
with a cocktail party with this hanging over him? In his mind's
eye he saw him wandering haunted from guest to guest with a
cocktail in his hand and his grosses up twenty-seven thousand.

"So I came to you, Monroe. I never saw a situation where
you didn't know a way out. I said to myself: even if he advises
me to kill myself, I'll ask Monroe."

The buzzer sounded on Stahr's desk – he switched on the
dictagraph and heard Miss Doolan's voice.

"Five minutes, Mr Stahr."

"I'm sorry," said Stahr. "I'll need a few minutes more."

"Five hundred girls marched to my house from the high
school," the actor said gloomily, "and I stood behind the curtains and watched them. I couldn't go out."

"You sit down," said Stahr. "We'll take plenty of time and
talk this over."

In the outer office, two members of the conference group had
already waited ten minutes – Wylie White and Jane Meloney.
The latter was a dried-up little blonde of fifty, about whom one
could hear the fifty assorted opinions of Hollywood – "a sentimental dope", "the best writer on construction in Hollywood",
"a veteran", "that old hack", "the smartest woman on the lot",

"the cleverest plagiarist in the biz" – and, of course, in addition she was variously described as a nymphomaniac, a virgin, a pushover, a lesbian and a faithful wife. Without being an old maid, she was, like most self-made women, rather old-maidish. She had ulcers of the stomach, and her salary was over a hundred thousand a year. A complicated treatise could be written on whether she was "worth it", or more than that or nothing at all. Her value lay in such ordinary assets as the bare fact that she was a woman and adaptable, quick and trustworthy, "knew the game" and was without egotism. She had been a great friend of Minna's, and over a period of years Stahr had managed to stifle what amounted to a sharp physical revulsion.

She and Wylie waited in silence – occasionally addressing a remark to Miss Doolan. Every few minutes Reinmund, the supervisor, called up from his office, where he and Broaca, the director, were waiting. After ten minutes Stahr's button went on, and Miss Doolan called Reinmund and Broaca; simultaneously Stahr and the actor came out of Stahr's office with Stahr holding the man's arm. He was so wound up now that when Wylie White asked him how he was he opened his mouth and began to tell him then and there.

"Oh, I've had an awful time," he said, but Stahr interrupted sharply.

"No, you haven't. Now you go along and do the role the way I said."

"Thank you, Monroe."

Jane Meloney looked after him without speaking.

"Somebody been catching flies on him?" she asked – a phrase for stealing scenes.

"I'm sorry I kept you waiting," Stahr said. "Come on in."

* * *

It was noon already and the conferees were entitled to exactly an hour of Stahr's time. No less, for such a conference could only be interrupted by a director who was held up in his shooting; seldom much more, because every eight days the company must release a production as complex and costly as Reinhardt's *Miracle*.*

Occasionally, less often than five years ago, Stahr would work all through the night on a single picture. But after such a spree he felt badly for days. If he could go from problem to problem, there was a certain rebirth of vitality with each change. And like those sleepers who can wake whenever they wish, he had set his psychological clock to run one hour.

The cast assembled included, besides the writers, Reinmund, one of the most favoured of the supervisors, and John Broaca, the picture's director.

Broaca, on the surface, was all engineer – large and without nerves, quietly resolute, popular. He was an ignoramus, and Stahr often caught him making the same scenes over and over – one scene about a rich young girl occurred in all his pictures with the same action, the same business. A bunch of large dogs entered the room and jumped around the girl. Later the girl went to a stable and slapped a horse on the rump. The explanation was probably not Freudian: more likely that at a drab moment in youth he had looked through a fence and seen a beautiful girl with dogs and horses. As a trademark for glamour it was stamped on his brain for ever.

Reinmund was a handsome young opportunist with a fairly good education. Originally a man of some character, he was being daily forced by his anomalous position into devious ways of acting and thinking. He was a bad man now, as men go. At thirty he had none of the virtues which either gentile Americans or Jews are taught to think admirable. But he got his pictures out in time and, by manifesting an almost homosexual fixation on Stahr, seemed to have dulled Stahr's usual acuteness. Stahr liked him – considered him a good all-round man.

Wylie White, of course, in any country would have been recognizable as an intellectual of the second order. He was civilized and voluble, both simple and acute, half dazed and half saturnine. His jealousy of Stahr showed only in unguarded flashes, and was mingled with admiration and even affection.

"The production date for this picture is two weeks from Saturday," said Stahr. "I think basically it's all right – much improved."

Reinmund and the two writers exchanged a glance of congratulation.

"Except for one thing," said Stahr, thoughtfully. "I don't see why it should be produced at all, and I've decided to put it away."

There was a moment of shocked silence – and then murmurs of protest, stricken queries.

"It's not your fault," Stahr said. "I thought there was something there that wasn't there – that was all." He hesitated, looking regretfully at Reinmund: "It's too bad – it was a good play. We paid fifty thousand for it."

"What's the matter with it, Monroe?" asked Broaca bluntly.

"Well, it hardly seems worthwhile to go into it," said Stahr.

Reinmund and Wylie White were both thinking of the professional effect on them. Reinmund had two pictures to his account this year – but Wylie White needed a credit to start his comeback to the scene. Jane Meloney was watching Stahr closely from little skull-like eyes.

"Couldn't you give us some clue?" Reinmund asked. "This is a good deal of a blow, Monroe."

"I just wouldn't put Margaret Sullavan* in it," said Stahr. "Or Colman* either. I wouldn't advise them to play it—"

"Specifically, Monroe," begged Wylie White. "What didn't you like? The scenes? The dialogue? The humour? Construction?"

Stahr picked up the script from his desk, let it fall as if it were, physically, too heavy to handle.

"I don't like the people," he said. "I wouldn't like to meet them – if I knew they were going to be somewhere, I'd go somewhere else."

Reinmund smiled, but there was worry in his eyes.

"Well, that's a damning criticism," he said. "I thought the people were rather interesting."

"So did I," said Broaca. "I thought Em was very sympathetic."

"Did you?" asked Stahr sharply. "I could just barely believe she was alive. And when I came to the end, I said to myself, 'So what?'"

"There must be something to do," Reinmund said. "Naturally we feel bad about this. This is the structure we agreed on—"

"But it's not the story," said Stahr. "I've told you many times that the first thing I decide is the *kind* of story I want. We change in every other regard, but once that is set we've got to work towards it with every line and movement. This is not the kind of story I want. The story we bought had shine and glow

– it was a happy story. This is all full of doubt and hesitation. The hero and heroine stop loving each other over trifles – then they start up again over trifles. After the first sequence, you don't care if she never sees him again or he her."

"That's my fault," said Wylie suddenly. "You see, Monroe, I don't think stenographers have the same dumb admiration for their bosses they had in 1929. They've been laid off – they've seen their bosses jittery. The world has moved on, that's all."

Stahr looked at him impatiently, gave a short nod.

"That's not under discussion," he said. "The premiss of this story is that the girl did have a dumb admiration for her boss, if you want to call it that. And there wasn't any evidence that he'd ever been jittery. When you make her doubt him in any way, you have a different kind of story. Or rather you haven't anything at all. These people are extroverts – get that straight – and I want them to extrovert all over the lot. When I want to do a Eugene O'Neill play,* I'll buy one."

Jane Meloney, who had never taken her eyes off Stahr, knew it was going to be all right now. If he had really been going to abandon the picture, he wouldn't have gone at it like this. She had been in this game longer than any of them except Broaca, with whom she had had a three-day affair twenty years ago.

Stahr turned to Reinmund.

"You ought to have understood from the casting, Reiny, what kind of a picture I wanted. I started marking the lines that Carroll and McMurray* couldn't say and got tired of it. Remember this in the future – if I order a limousine, I want that kind of car. And the fastest midget racer you ever saw wouldn't do. Now –" he looked around – "shall we go any farther? Now that I've told you I don't even like the kind of picture this is? Shall we go on? We've got two weeks. At the end of that time I'm going to put Carroll and McMurray into this or something else – is it worthwhile?"

"Well, naturally," said Reinmund, "I think it is. I feel bad about this. I should have warned Wylie. I thought he had some good ideas."

"Monroe's right," said Broaca bluntly. "I felt this was wrong all the time, but I couldn't put my finger on it."

Wylie and Rose looked at him contemptuously and exchanged a glance.

"Do you writers think you can get hot on it again?" asked Stahr, not unkindly. "Or shall I try somebody fresh?"

"I'd like another shot," said Wylie.

"How about you, Jane?"

She nodded briefly.

"What do you think of the girl?" asked Stahr.

"Well – naturally I'm prejudiced in her favour."

"You better forget it," said Stahr warningly. "Ten million Americans would put thumbs down on that girl if she walked on the screen. We've got an hour and twenty-five minutes on the screen – you show a woman being unfaithful to a man for one third of that time and you've given the impression that she's one third whore."

"Is that a big proportion?" asked Jane slyly, and they laughed.

"It is for me," said Stahr thoughtfully, "even if it wasn't for the Hays* office. If you want to paint a scarlet letter on her back, it's all right, but that's another story. Not this story. This is a future wife and mother. However – *however*" –

He pointed his pencil at Wylie White.

– "this has as much passion as that Oscar on my desk."

"What the hell!" said Wylie. "She's full of it. Why she goes to—"

"She's loose enough," said Stahr. "But that's all. There's one scene in the play better than all this you cooked up, and you've left it out. When she's trying to make the time pass by changing her watch."

"It didn't seem to fit," Wylie apologized.

"Now," said Stahr, "I've got about fifty ideas. I'm going to call Miss Doolan." He pressed a button. "And if there's anything you don't understand, speak up…"

Miss Doolan slid in almost imperceptibly. Pacing the floor swiftly, Stahr began. In the first place he wanted to tell them what kind of girl she was – what kind of a girl he approved of here. She was a perfect girl, with a few small faults as in the play, but a perfect girl, not because the public wanted her that way but because it was the kind of girl that he, Stahr, liked to see in this sort of picture. Was that clear? It was no character role. She stood for health, vitality, ambition and love. What gave the play its importance was entirely a situation in which she found herself. She became possessed of a secret that affected a great many lives. There was a right thing and a wrong thing to do – at first it was not plain which was which, but when it was, she went right away and did it. That was the kind of story this was – thin, clean and shining. No doubts.

"She has never heard the word labour troubles," he said with a sigh. "She might be living in 1929. Is it plain what kind of girl I want?"

"It's very plain, Monroe."

"Now about the things she does," said Stahr. "At all times, at all moments when she is on the screen in our sight, she wants to sleep with Ken Willard. Is that plain, Wylie?"

"Passionately plain."

"Whatever she does, it is in place of sleeping with Ken Willard. If she walks down the street she is walking to sleep with Ken Willard, if she eats her food it is to give her strength to sleep with Ken Willard. *But* at no time do you give the impression that she would even consider sleeping with Ken Willard unless they were properly sanctified. I'm ashamed of having to tell you these kindergarten facts, but they have somehow leaked out of the story."

He opened the script and began to go through it page by page. Miss Doolan's notes would be typed in quintuplicate and given to them, but Jane Meloney made notes of her own. Broaca put his hand up to his half-closed eyes – he could remember "when a director was something out here", when writers were gag men or eager and ashamed young reporters full of whiskey – a director was all there was then. No supervisor – no Stahr.

He started wide awake as he heard his name.

"It would be nice, John, if you could put the boy on a pointed roof and let him walk around and keep the camera on him. You might get a nice feeling – not danger, not suspense, not pointing for anything – a kid on the roof in the morning."

Broaca brought himself back in the room.

"All right," he said. "Just an element of danger."

"Not exactly," said Stahr. "He doesn't start to fall off the roof. Break into the next scene with it."

"Through the window," suggested Jane Meloney. "He could climb in his sister's window."

"That's a good transition," said Stahr. "Right into the diary scene."

Broaca was wide awake now.

"I'll shoot up at him," he said. "Let him go away from the camera. Just a fixed shot from quite a distance – let him go away from the camera. Don't follow him. Pick him up in a close shot and let him go away again. No attention on him except against the whole roof and the sky." He liked the shot – it was a director's shot that didn't come up on every page any more. He might use a crane – it would be cheaper in the end than building the roof on the ground with a process sky. That was one thing about Stahr – the literal sky was the limit. He had worked with Jews too long to believe legends that they were small with money.

"In the third sequence have him hit the priest," Stahr said.

"What!" Wylie cried. "And have the Catholics on our neck."

"I've talked to Joe Breen.* Priests have been hit. It doesn't reflect on them."

His quiet voice ran on – stopped abruptly as Miss Doolan glanced at the clock.

"Is that too much to do before Monday?" he asked Wylie.

Wylie looked at Jane and she looked back, not even bothering to nod. He saw their weekend melting away, but he was a different man from when he entered the room. When you were paid fifteen hundred a week, emergency work was one thing you did not skimp, not when your picture was threatened. As a "freelance" writer Wylie had failed from lack of caring, but here was Stahr to care for all of them. The effect would not wear off when he left the office – nor anywhere within the walls of the lot. He felt a great purposefulness. The mixture of common sense, wise sensibility, theatrical ingenuity and a certain half-naive conception of the common weal which Stahr had just stated aloud, inspired him to do his part, to get his block of stone in place, even if the effort were foredoomed, the result as dull as a pyramid.

Out of the window Jane Meloney watched the trickle streaming towards the commissary. She would have her lunch in her office and knit a few rows while it came. The man was coming at one fifteen with the French perfume smuggled over the Mexican border. That was no sin – it was like prohibition.

Broaca watched as Reinmund fawned upon Stahr. He sensed that Reinmund was on his way up. He received seven hundred and fifty a week for his partial authority over directors, writers and stars, who got much more. He wore a pair of cheap English shoes he had bought near the Beverly Wilshire, and Broaca hoped they hurt his feet, but soon now he would order his shoes from Peel's and put away his little green Alpine hat with a feather. Broaca was years ahead of him. He had a fine record in the War, but he had never felt quite the same with himself since he had let Ike Franklin strike him in the face with his open hand.

There was smoke in the room, and behind it, behind his great desk, Stahr was withdrawing further and further, in all courtesy, still giving Reinmund an ear and Miss Doolan an ear. The conference was over.

* * *

"Mr Marcus calling from New York," said Miss Doolan.

"What do you mean?" demanded Stahr. "Why, I saw him here last night."

"Well, he's on the phone – it's a New York call and Miss Jacobs's voice. It's his office."

Stahr laughed.

"I'm seeing him at lunch," he said. "There's no aeroplane fast enough to take him there."

Miss Doolan returned to the phone. Stahr lingered to hear the outcome.

"It's all right," said Miss Doolan presently. "It was a mistake. Mr Marcus called east this morning to tell them about the quake and the flood on the back lot, and it seems he asked them to ask you about it. It was a new secretary who didn't understand Mr Marcus. I think she got mixed up."

"I think she did," said Stahr grimly.

Prince Agge did not understand either of them but, looking for the fabulous, he felt it was something triumphantly American. Mr Marcus, whose quarters could be seen across the way, had called his New York office to ask Stahr about the flood. The Prince imagined some intricate relationship without realizing that the transaction had taken place entirely within the once brilliant steel-trap mind of Mr Marcus, which was intermittently slipping.

"I think she was a very new secretary," repeated Stahr. "Any other messages?"

"Mr Robinson called in," Miss Doolan said, as she started for the commissary. "One of the women told him her name, but he's forgotten it – he thinks it was Smith or Brown or Jones."

"That's a great help."

"And he remembers she says she just moved to Los Angeles."

"I remember she had a silver belt," Stahr said, "with stars cut out of it."

"I'm still trying to find out more about Pete Zavras. I talked to his wife."

"What did she say?"

"Oh, they've had an awful time – given up their house – she's been sick…"

"Is the eye trouble hopeless?"

"She didn't seem to know anything about the state of his eyes. She didn't even know he was going blind."

"That's funny."

He thought about it on the way to luncheon, but it was as confusing as the actor's trouble this morning. Troubles about people's health didn't seem within his range – he gave no thought to his own. In the lane beside the commissary he stepped back as an open electric truck crammed with girls in the bright costumes of the Regency came rolling in from the back lot. The dresses were fluttering in the wind, the young painted faces looked at him curiously, and he smiled as it went by.

* * *

Eleven men and their guest, Prince Agge, sat at lunch in the private dining room of the studio commissary. They were the money men – they were the rulers – and unless there was a guest, they ate in broken silence, sometimes asking questions about each other's wives and children, sometimes discharging a single absorption from the forefront of their consciousness. Eight out of the ten were Jews; five of the ten were foreign-born, including a Greek and an Englishman; and they had all known each other for a long time: there was a rating in the group, from old Marcus down to old Leanbaum, who had bought the most fortunate block of stock in the business and never was allowed to spend over a million a year producing.

Old Marcus still managed to function with disquieting resilience. Some never-atrophying instinct warned him of danger, of gangings-up against him – he was never so dangerous himself as when others considered him surrounded. His grey face had attained such immobility that even those who were accustomed to watch the reflex of the inner corner of his eye could no longer see it. Nature had grown a little white whisker there to conceal it; his armour was complete.

As he was the oldest, Stahr was the youngest of the group – not by many years at this date, though he had first sat with most of these men when he was a boy wonder of twenty-two. Then, more than now, he had been a money man among money men. Then he had been able to figure costs in his head with a speed and accuracy that dazzled them – for they were not wizards or even experts in that regard, despite the popular conception of Jews in finance. Most of them owed their success to different and incompatible qualities. But in a group a tradition carries along the less adept, and they were content to look at Stahr for the sublimated auditing, and experience a sort of glow as if they had done it themselves, like rooters at a football game.

Stahr, as will presently be seen, had grown away from that particular gift, though it was always there.

Prince Agge sat between Stahr and Mort Fleishacker, the company lawyer, and across from Joe Popolos, the theatre owner. He was hostile to Jews in a vague, general way that he tried to cure himself of. As a turbulent man, serving his time in the Foreign Legion, he thought that Jews were too fond of their own skins. But he was willing to concede that they might be different in America under different circumstances, and certainly he found Stahr was much of a man in every way. For the rest – he thought most businessmen were dull dogs – for final reference he reverted always to the blood of Bernadotte* in his veins.

My father – I will call him Mr Brady, as Prince Agge did when he told me of this luncheon – was worried about a picture, and when Leanbaum went out early, he came up and took his chair opposite.

"How about the South America picture idea, Monroe?" he asked.

Prince Agge noticed a blink of attention towards them as distinct as if a dozen pairs of eyelashes had made the sound of batting wings. Then silence again.

"We're going ahead with it," said Stahr.

"With that same budget?" Brady asked.

Stahr nodded.

"It's out of proportion," said Brady. "There won't be any miracle in these bad times – no *Hell's Angels* or *Ben Hur*,* when you throw it away and get it back."

Probably the attack was planned, for Popolos, the Greek, took up the matter in a sort of double talk.

"It's not adoptable, Monroe, in as we wish adopt to this times in as it changes. It what could be done as we run the gamut of prosperity is scarcely conceptuable now."

"What do you think, Mr Marcus?" asked Stahr.

All eyes followed his down the table, but, as if forewarned, Mr Marcus had already signalled his private waiter behind him that he wished to rise, and was even now in a basket-like position in the waiter's arms. He looked at them with such helplessness that it was hard to realize that in the evenings he sometimes went dancing with his young Canadian girl.

"Monroe is our production genius," he said. "I count upon Monroe and lean heavily upon him. I have not seen the flood myself."

There was a moment of silence as he moved from the room.

"There's not a two-million-dollar gross in the country now," said Brady.

"Is not," agreed Popolos. "Even as if so you could grab them by the head and push them by and in, is not."

"Probably not," agreed Stahr. He paused as if to make sure that all were listening. "I think we can count on a million and a quarter from the roadshow. Perhaps a million and a half altogether. And a quarter of a million abroad."

Again there was silence – this time puzzled, a little confused. Over his shoulder Stahr asked the waiter to be connected with his office on the phone.

"But your budget?" said Fleishacker. "Your budget is seventeen hundred and fifty thousand, I understand. And your expectations only add up to that without profits."

"Those aren't my expectations," said Stahr. "We're not sure of more than a million and a half."

The room had grown so motionless that Prince Agge could hear a grey chunk of ash fall from a cigar in mid air. Fleishacker started to speak, his face fixed with amazement, but a phone had been handed over Stahr's shoulder.

"Your office, Mr Stahr."

"Oh, yes – oh, hello, Miss Doolan. I've figured it out about Zavras. It's one of those lousy rumours – I'll bet my shirt on it… Oh, you did. Good… good. Now here's what to do: send him to my oculist this afternoon – Dr John Kennedy – and have him get a report and have it photostated – you understand?"

He hung up – turned with a touch of passion to the table at large.

"Did any of you ever hear a story that Pete Zavras was going blind?"

There were a couple of nods. But most of those present were poised breathlessly on whether Stahr had slipped on his figures a minute before.

"It's pure bunk. He says he's never even been to an oculist – never knew why the studios turned against him," said Stahr. "Somebody didn't like him or somebody talked too much, and he's been out of work for a year."

There was a conventional murmur of sympathy. Stahr signed the cheque and made as though to get up.

"Excuse me, Monroe," said Fleishacker persistently, while Brady and Popolos watched. "I'm fairly new here, and perhaps I fail to comprehend implicitly and explicitly." He was talking fast, but the veins on his forehead bulged with pride at the big words from NYU. "Do I understand you to say you expect to gross a quarter million short of your budget?"

"It's a quality picture," said Stahr with assumed innocence.

It had dawned on them all now, but they still felt there was a trick in it. Stahr really thought it would make money. No one in his senses—

"For two years we've played safe," said Stahr. "It's time we made a picture that'll lose some money. Write it off as goodwill – this'll bring in new customers."

Some of them still thought he meant it was a flyer and a favourable one, but he left them in no doubt.

"It'll lose money," he said as he stood up, his jaw just slightly out and his eyes smiling and shining. "It would be a bigger miracle than *Hell's Angels* if it broke even. But we have a certain duty to the public, as Pat Brady has said at Academy dinners. It's a good thing for the production schedule to slip in a picture that'll lose money."

He nodded at Prince Agge. As the latter made his bows quickly, he tried to take in with a last glance the general effect of what Stahr had said, but he could tell nothing. The eyes, not so much downcast as fixed upon an indefinite distance just above the table, were all blinking quickly now, but there was not a whisper in the room.

* * *

Coming out of the private dining room they passed through a corner of the commissary proper. Prince Agge drank it in – eagerly. It was gay with gypsies and with citizens and soldiers, with the sideburns and braided coats of the First Empire. From a little distance they were men who lived and walked a hundred years ago, and Agge wondered how he and the men of his time would look as extras in some future costume picture.

Then he saw Abraham Lincoln, and his whole feeling suddenly changed. He had been brought up in the dawn of Scandinavian socialism when Nicolay's biography* was much read. He had been told Lincoln was a great man whom he should admire, and he hated him instead, because he was forced upon him. But now seeing him sitting here, his legs crossed, his kindly face fixed on a forty-cent dinner, including dessert, his shawl wrapped around him as if to protect himself from the erratic air-cooling – now Prince Agge, who was in America at last, stared as a tourist at the mummy of Lenin in the Kremlin. This, then, was Lincoln. Stahr had walked on far ahead of him, turned, waiting for him – but still Agge stared.

This, then, he thought, was what they all meant to be.

Lincoln suddenly raised a triangle of pie and jammed it in his mouth, and, a little frightened, Prince Agge hurried to join Stahr.

"I hope you're getting what you want," said Stahr, feeling he had neglected him. "We'll have some rushes in half an hour and then you can go onto as many sets as you want."

"I should rather stay with you," said Prince Agge.

"I'll see what there is for me," said Stahr. "Then we'll go on together."

There was the Japanese consul on the release of a spy story which might offend the national sensibilities of Japan. There were phone calls and telegrams. There was some further information from Robby.

"Now he remembers the name of the woman. He's sure it was Smith," said Miss Doolan. "He asked her if she wanted to come on the lot and get some dry shoes, and she said no – so she can't sue."

"That's pretty bad for a total recall – 'Smith'. That's a great help." He thought a moment: "Ask the phone company for a list of Smiths that have taken new phones here in the last month. Call them all."

"All right."

Chapter 4

"HOW ARE YOU, MONROE?" said Red Ridingwood. "I'm glad you came down."

Stahr walked past him, heading across the great stage towards the set of a brilliant room that would be used tomorrow. Director Ridingwood followed, realizing after a moment that however fast he walked Stahr managed to be a step or two ahead. He recognized the indication of displeasure – he had used it himself. He had had his own studio once and he had used everything. There was no stop Stahr could pull that would surprise him. His task was the delivery of situations, and Stahr by effective business could not outplay him on his own grounds. Goldwyn had once interfered with him, and Ridingwood had led Goldwyn into trying to act out a part in front of fifty people – with the result that he had anticipated: his own authority had been restored.

Stahr reached the brilliant set and stopped.

"It's no good," said Ridingwood. "No imagination. I don't care how you light it—"

"Why did you call me about it?" Stahr asked, standing close to him. "Why didn't you take it up with Art?"

"I didn't ask you to come down, Monroe."

"You wanted to be your own supervisor."

"I'm sorry, Monroe," said Ridingwood patiently, "but I didn't ask you to come down."

Stahr turned suddenly and walked back towards the camera set-up. The eyes and open mouths of a group of visitors moved momentarily off the heroine of the picture, took in Stahr, and then moved vacantly back to the heroine again. They were Knights of Columbus.* They had seen the host carried in procession, but this was the dream made flesh.

Stahr stopped beside her chair. She wore a low gown which displayed the bright eczema of her chest and back. Before each take, the blemished surface was plastered over with an emollient, which was removed immediately after the take. Her hair was of the colour and viscosity of drying blood, but there was starlight that actually photographed in her eyes.

Before Stahr could speak, he heard a helpful voice behind him: "She's radiunt. Absolutely radiunt."

It was an assistant director, and the intention was delicate compliment. The actress was being complimented so that she did not have to strain her poor skin to bend and hear. Stahr was being complimented for having her under contract. Ridingwood was being remotely complimented.

"Everything all right?" Stahr asked her pleasantly.

"Oh, it's fine," she agreed. "Except for the —ing publicity men."

He winked at her gently.

"We'll keep them away," he said.

Her name had become currently synonymous with the expression "bitch". Presumably she had modelled herself after one of those queens in the Tarzan comics who rule mysteriously over a nation of blacks. She regarded the rest of the world as black. She was a necessary evil, borrowed for a single picture.

Ridingwood walked with Stahr towards the door of the stage.

"Everything's all right," the director said. "She's as good as she can be."

They were out of hearing range, and Stahr stopped suddenly and looked at Red with blazing eyes.

"You've been photographing crap," he said. "Do you know what she reminds me of in the rushes? 'Miss Foodstuffs'."

"I'm trying to get the best performance—"

"Come along with me," said Stahr abruptly.

"With you? Shall I tell them to rest?"

"Leave it as it is," said Stahr, pushing the padded outer door.

His car and chauffeur waited outside. Minutes were precious most days.

"Get in," said Stahr.

Red knew now it was serious. He even knew all at once what was the matter. The girl had got the whip hand on him the first day with her cold lashing tongue. He was a peace-loving man and he had let her walk through her part cold, rather than cause trouble.

Stahr spoke into his thoughts.

"You can't handle her," he said. "I told you what I wanted. I wanted her *mean* – and she comes out bored. I'm afraid we'll have to call it off, Red."

"The picture?"

"No. I'm putting Harley on it."

"All right, Monroe."

"I'm sorry, Red. We'll try something else another time."

The car drew up in front of Stahr's office.

"Shall I finish this take?" said Red.

"It's being done now," said Stahr grimly. "Harley's in there."

"What the hell—"

"He went in when we came out. I had him read the script last night."

"Now listen, Monroe—"

"It's my busy day, Red," said Stahr tersely. "You lost interest about three days ago."

It was a sorry mess, Ridingwood thought. It meant he would have slight, very slight loss of position – it probably meant that he could not have a third wife just now as he had planned. There wasn't even the satisfaction of raising a row about it – if you disagreed with Stahr, you did not advertise it. Stahr was his world's great customer, who was always – almost always – right.

"How about my coat?" he asked suddenly. "I left it over a chair on the set."

"I know you did," said Stahr. "Here it is."

He was trying so hard to be charitable about Ridingwood's lapse that he had forgotten that he had it in his hand.

* * *

"Mr Stahr's Projection Room" was a miniature picture theatre with four rows of overstuffed chairs. In front of the front row ran long tables with dim lamps, buzzers and telephones. Against the wall was an upright piano, left there since the early days of sound. The room had been redecorated and reupholstered only a year before, but already it was ragged again with work and hours.

Here Stahr sat at two thirty and again at six thirty watching the lengths of film taken during the day. There was often a savage tensity about the occasion – he was dealing with faits accomplis – the net results of months of buying, planning, writing and rewriting, casting, constructing, lighting, rehearsing and shooting – the fruit of brilliant hunches or of counsels of despair, of lethargy, conspiracy and sweat. At this point the tortuous manoeuvre was staged and in suspension – there were reports from the battle line.

Besides Stahr, there were present the representatives of all technical departments, together with the supervisors and unit managers of the pictures concerned. The directors did not appear at these showings – officially because their work was considered done, actually because few punches were pulled here as money ran out in silver spools. There had evolved a delicate staying-away.

The staff was already assembled. Stahr came in and took his place quickly, and the murmur of conversation died away. As he sat back and drew his thin knee up beside him in the chair, the lights in the room went out. There was the flare of a match in the back row – then silence.

On the screen a troop of French Canadians pushed their canoes up a rapids. The scene had been photographed in a studio tank, and at the end of each take, after the director's voice could be heard saying "Cut", the actors on the screen relaxed and wiped their brows and sometimes laughed hilariously – and the water in the tank stopped flowing and the illusion ceased. Except to name his choice from each set of takes and to remark that it was "a good process", Stahr made no comment.

The next scene, still in the rapids, called for dialogue between the Canadian girl (Claudette Colbert)* and the *coureur du bois** (Ronald Colman), with her looking down at him from a canoe. After a few strips had run through, Stahr spoke up suddenly.

"Has the tank been dismantled?"

"Yes, sir."

"Monroe – they needed it for—"

Stahr cut in peremptorily.

"Have it set up again right away. Let's have that second take again."

The lights went on momentarily. One of the unit managers left his chair and came and stood in front of Stahr.

"A beautifully acted scene thrown away," raged Stahr quietly. "It wasn't centred. The camera was set up so it caught the beautiful top of Claudette's head all the time she was talking. That's just what we want, isn't it? That's just what people go to see – the top of a beautiful girl's head. Tell Tim he could have saved wear and tear by using her stand-in."

The lights went out again. The unit manager squatted by Stahr's chair to be out of the way. The take was run again.

"Do you see now?" asked Stahr. "And there's a hair in the picture – there on the right, see it? Find out if it's in the projector or the film."

At the very end of the take, Claudette Colbert slowly lifted her head, revealing her great liquid eyes.

"That's what we should have had all the way," said Stahr. "She gave a fine performance too. See if you can fit it in tomorrow or late this afternoon."

Pete Zavras would not have made a slip like that. There were not six camera men in the industry you could entirely trust.

The lights went on; the supervisor and unit manager for that picture went out.

"Monroe, this stuff was shot yesterday – it came through late last night."

The room darkened. On the screen appeared the head of Shiva, immense and imperturbable, oblivious to the fact that in a few hours it was to be washed away in a flood. Around it milled a crowd of the faithful.

"When you take that scene again," said Stahr suddenly, "put a couple of little kids up on top. You better check about whether it's reverent or not, but I think it's all right. Kids'll do anything."

"Yes, Monroe."

A silver belt with stars cut out of it... Smith, Jones or Brown... Personal – will the woman with the silver belt who—

With another picture the scene shifted to New York, a gangster story, and suddenly Stahr became restive.

"That scene's trash," he called suddenly in the darkness. "It's badly written, it's miscast, it accomplishes nothing. Those types aren't tough. They look like a lot of dressed-up lollipops – what the hell is the matter, Lee?"

"The scene was written on the set this morning," said Lee Kapper. "Burton wanted to get all the stuff on Stage 6."

"Well – it's trash. And so is this one. There's no use printing stuff like that. She doesn't believe what she's saying – neither does Cary.* 'I love you' in a close-up – they'll cluck you out of the house! And the girl's overdressed."

In the darkness a signal was given, the projector stopped, the lights went on. The room waited in utter silence. Stahr's face was expressionless.

"Who wrote the scene?" he asked after a minute.

"Wylie White."

"Is he sober?"

"Sure he is."

Stahr considered.

"Put about four writers on that scene tonight," he said. "See who we've got. Is Sidney Howard* here yet?"

"He got in this morning."

"Talk to him about it. Explain to him what I want there. The girl is in deadly terror – she's stalling. It's as simple as that. People don't have three emotions at once. And Kapper..."

The art director leant forward out of the second row.

"Yeah."

"There's something the matter with that set."

There were little glances exchanged all over the room.

"What is it, Monroe?"

"You tell *me*," said Stahr. "It's crowded. It doesn't carry your eye out. It looks cheap."

"It wasn't."

"I know it wasn't. There's not much the matter, but there's something. Go over and take a look tonight. It may be too much furniture – or the wrong kind. Perhaps a window would help. Couldn't you force the perspective in that hall a little more?"

"I'll see what I can do." Kapper edged his way out of the row, looking at his watch.

"I'll have to get at it right away," he said. "I'll work tonight and we'll put it up in the morning."

"All right. Lee, you can shoot around those scenes, can't you?"

"I think so, Monroe."

"I take the blame for this. Have you got the fight stuff?"

"Coming up now."

Stahr nodded. Kapper hurried out, and the room went dark again. On the screen four men staged a terrific socking match in a cellar. Stahr laughed.

"Look at Tracy,"* he said. "Look at him go down after that guy. I bet he's been in a few."

The men fought over and over. Always the same fight. Always at the end they faced each other smiling, sometimes touching the opponent in a friendly gesture on the shoulder. The only one in danger was the stunt man, a pug who could have murdered the other three. He was in danger only if they swung wild and didn't follow the blows he had taught them. Even so, the youngest actor was afraid for his face and the director had covered his flinches with ingenious angles and interpositions.

And then two men met endlessly in a door, recognized each other, and went on. They met, they started, they went on.

Then a little girl read underneath a tree with a boy reading on a limb of the tree above. The little girl was bored and wanted to talk to the boy. He would pay no attention. The core of the apple he was eating fell on the little girl's head.

A voice spoke up out of the darkness:

"It's pretty long, isn't it, Monroe?"

"Not a bit," said Stahr. "It's nice. It has nice feeling."

"I just thought it was long."

"Sometimes ten feet can be too long – sometimes a scene two hundred feet long can be too short. I want to speak to the cutter before he touches this scene – this is something that'll be remembered in the picture."

The oracle had spoken. There was nothing to question or argue. Stahr must be right always, not most of the time, but always – or the structure would melt down like gradual butter.

Another hour passed. Dreams hung in fragments at the far end of the room, suffered analysis, passed – to be dreamt in crowds, or else discarded. The end was signalled by two tests, a character man and a girl. After the rushes, which had a tense rhythm of their own, the tests were smooth and finished; the observers settled in their chairs; Stahr's foot slipped to the floor. Opinions were welcome. One of the technical men let it be known that he would willingly cohabit with the girl; the rest were indifferent.

"Somebody sent up a test of that girl two years ago. She must be getting around – but she isn't getting any better. But the man's good. Can't we use him as the old Russian Prince in *Steppes*?"

"He *is* an old Russian Prince," said the casting director, "but he's ashamed of it. He's a Red. And that's one part he says he wouldn't play."

"It's the only part he could play," said Stahr.

The lights went on. Stahr rolled his gum into its wrapper and put it in an ashtray. He turned questioningly to his secretary.

"The processes on Stage 2," she said.

He looked in briefly at the processes, moving pictures taken against a background of other moving pictures by an ingenious device. There was a meeting in Marcus's office on the subject of *Manon** with a happy ending, and Stahr had his say on that as he had had before – it had been making money without a happy ending for a century and a half. He was obdurate – at this time in the afternoon he was at his most fluent and the opposition faded into another subject: they would lend a dozen stars to the benefit for those the quake had made homeless at Long Beach. In a sudden burst of giving, five of them all at once made up a purse of twenty-five thousand dollars. They gave well, but not as poor men give. It was not charity.

At his office there was word from the oculist to whom he had sent Pete Zavras that the camera man's eyes were 19–20: approximately perfect. He had written a letter that Zavras was having photostated. Stahr walked around his office cockily while Miss Doolan admired him. Prince Agge had dropped in to thank him for his afternoon on the sets and, while they talked, a cryptic word came from a supervisor that some writers named Tarleton had "found out" and were about to quit.

"These are good writers," Stahr explained to Prince Agge, "and we don't have good writers out here."

"Why, you can hire anyone!" exclaimed his visitor in surprise.

"Oh, we hire them, but when they get out here, they're not good writers – so we have to work with the material we have."

"Such as what?"

"Anybody that'll accept the system and stay decently sober – we have all sorts of people – disappointed poets, one-hit playwrights – college girls – we put them on an idea in pairs, and if it slows down, we put two more writers working behind them. I've had as many as three pairs working independently on the same idea."

"Do they like that?"

"Not if they know about it. They're not geniuses – none of them could make as much any other way. But these Tarletons are a husband-and-wife team from the East – pretty good playwrights. They've just found out they're not alone on the story and it shocks them – shocks their sense of unity – that's the word they'll use."

"But what does make the – the unity?"

Stahr hesitated – his face was grim except that his eyes twinkled.

"I'm the unity," he said. "Come and see us again."

He saw the Tarletons. He told them he liked their work, looking at Mrs Tarleton as if he could read her handwriting through the typescript. He told them kindly that he was taking them from the picture and putting them on another, where there was less pressure, more time. As he had half-expected, they begged to stay on the first picture, seeing a quicker credit, even though it was shared with others. The system was a shame, he admitted – gross, commercial, to be deplored. He had originated it – a fact that he did not mention.

When they had gone, Miss Doolan came in triumphant.

"Mr Stahr, the lady with the belt is on the phone."

Stahr walked into his office alone and sat down behind his desk and picked up the phone with a great sinking of his stomach. He did not know what he wanted. He had not thought about the matter as he had thought about the matter of Pete Zavras. At first he had only wanted to know if they were "professional" people, if the woman was an actress who had got herself up to look like Minna, as he had once had a young actress made up like Claudette Colbert and photographed her from the same angles.

"Hello," he said.

"Hello."

As he searched the short, rather surprised word for a vibration of last night, the feeling of terror began to steal over him, and he choked it off with an effort of will.

"Well – you were hard to find," he said. "*Smith* – and you moved here recently. That was all we had. And a silver belt."

"Oh, yes," the voice said, still uneasy, unpoised, "I had on a silver belt last night."

Now, where from here?

"Who *are* you?" the voice said, with a touch of flurried bourgeois dignity.

"My name is Monroe Stahr," he said.

A pause. It was a name that never appeared on the screen, and she seemed to have trouble placing it.

"Oh, yes – yes. You were the husband of Minna Davis."

"Yes."

Was it a trick? As the whole vision of last night came back to him – the very skin with that peculiar radiance, as if phosphorus had touched it – he thought whether it might not be a trick to reach him from somewhere. Not Minna and yet Minna. The curtains blew suddenly into the room, the papers whispered on his desk, and his heart cringed faintly at the intense reality of the day outside his window. If he could go out now this way, what would happen if he saw her again – the starry veiled expression, the mouth strongly formed for poor brave human laughter.

"I'd like to see you. Would you like to come to the studio?"

Again the hesitancy – then a blank refusal.

"Oh, I don't think I ought to. I'm awfully sorry."

This last was purely formal, a brush-off, a final axe. Ordinary skin-deep vanity came to Stahr's aid, adding persuasion to his urgency.

"I'd like to see you," he said. "There's a reason."

"Well – I'm afraid that—"

"Could I come and see you?"

A pause again, not from hesitation, he felt, but to assemble her answer.

"There's something you don't know," she said finally.

"Oh, you're probably married." He was impatient. "It has nothing to do with that. I asked you to come here openly – bring your husband if you have one."

"It's… it's quite impossible."

"Why?"

"I feel silly even talking to you, but your secretary insisted – I thought I'd dropped something in the flood last night and you'd found it."

"I want very much to see you for five minutes."

"To put me in the movies?"

"That wasn't my idea."

There was such a long pause that he thought he had offended her.

"Where could I meet you?" she asked unexpectedly.

"Here? At your house?"

"No – somewhere outside."

Suddenly Stahr could think of no place. His own house – a restaurant. Where did people meet? A house of assignation, a cocktail bar?

"I'll meet you somewhere at nine o'clock," she said.

"That's impossible, I'm afraid."

"Then never mind."

"All right, then, nine o'clock, but can we make it near here? There's a drugstore on Wilshire…"

* * *

It was a quarter to six. There were two men outside who had come every day at this time only to be postponed.

This was an hour of fatigue – the men's business was not so important that it must be seen to, nor so insignificant that it could be ignored. So he postponed it again and sat motionless at his desk for a moment, thinking about Russia. Not so much about Russia as about the picture about Russia which would consume a hopeless half-hour presently. He knew there were many stories about Russia, not to mention The Story, and he had employed a squad of writers and research men for over a year, but all the stories involved had the wrong feel. He felt it could be told in terms of the American thirteen states, but it kept coming out different, in new terms that opened unpleasant possibilities and problems. He considered he was very fair to Russia – he had no desire to make anything but a sympathetic picture, but it kept turning into a headache.

"Mr Stahr – Mr Drummon's outside, and Mr Kirstoff and Mrs Cornhill, about the Russian picture."

"All right – send them in."

Afterwards from six thirty to seven thirty he watched the afternoon rushes. Except for his engagement with the girl, he would ordinarily have spent the early evening in the projection room or the dubbing room, but it had been a late night with the earthquake, and he decided to go to dinner. Coming in through his front office, he found Pete Zavras waiting, his arm in a sling.

"You are the Aeschylus and the Diogenes of the moving picture," said Zavras simply. "Also the Asclepius and the Menander."*

He bowed.

"Who are they?" asked Stahr smiling.

"They are my countrymen."

"I didn't know you made pictures in Greece."

"You're joking with me, Monroe," said Zavras. "I want to say you are as dandy a fellow as they come. You have saved me one hundred per cent."

"You feel all right now?"

"My arm is nothing. It feels like someone kisses me there. It was worth doing what I did, if this is the outcome."

"How did you happen to do it here?" Stahr asked curiously.

"Before the Delphic oracle," said Zavras. "The Oedipus who solved the riddle. I wish I had my hands on the son-of-a-bitch who started the story."

"You make me sorry I didn't get an education," said Stahr.

"It isn't worth a damn," said Pete. "I took my baccalaureate in Salonika and look how I ended up."

"Not quite," said Stahr.

"If you want anybody's throat cut anytime day or night," said Zavras, "my number is in the book."

Stahr closed his eyes and opened them again. Zavras's silhouette had blurred a little against the sun. He hung on to the table behind him and said in an ordinary voice.

"Good luck, Pete."

The room was almost black, but he made his feet move, following a pattern, into his office and waited till the door clicked shut before he felt for the pills. The water decanter clattered against the table; the glass clacked. He sat down in a big chair, waiting for the Benzedrine to take effect before he went to dinner.

* * *

As Stahr walked back from the commissary, a hand waved at him from an open roadster. From the heads showing over the back he recognized a young actor and his girl, and watched them disappear through the gate, already part of the summer twilight. Little by little he was losing the feel of such things, until it seemed that Minna had taken their poignancy with her; his appreciation of splendour was fading so that presently the luxury of eternal mourning would depart. A childish association of Minna with the material Heavens made him, when he reached his office, order out his roadster for the first time this year. The big limousine seemed heavy with remembered conferences or exhausted sleep.

Leaving the studio, he was still tense, but the open car pulled the summer evening up close, and he looked at it. There was a moon down at the end of the boulevard, and it was a good illusion that it was a different moon every evening, every year. Other lights shone in Hollywood since Minna's death: in the open markets lemons and grapefruit and green apples slanted a misty glare into the street. Ahead of him the stop signal of a car winked violet and at another crossing he watched it wink again. Everywhere floodlights raked the sky. On an empty corner two mysterious men moved a gleaming drum in pointless arcs over the heavens.

In the drugstore a woman stood by the candy counter. She was tall, almost as tall as Stahr, and embarrassed. Obviously it was a situation for her, and if Stahr had not looked as he did – most considerate and polite – she would not have gone through with it. They said hello, and walked out without another word, scarcely a glance – yet before they reached the kerb Stahr knew: this was just exactly a pretty American woman and nothing more – no beauty like Minna.

"Where are we going?" she asked. "I thought there'd be a chauffeur. Never mind – I'm a good boxer."

"Boxer?"

"That didn't sound very polite." She forced a smile. "But you people are supposed to be such *horrors*."

The conception of himself as sinister amused Stahr – then suddenly it failed to amuse him.

"Why did you want to see me?" she asked as she got in.

He stood motionless, wanting to tell her to get out immediately. But she had relaxed in the car, and he knew the unfortunate situation was of his own making – he shut his teeth and walked round to get in. The street lamp fell full upon her face, and it was difficult to believe that this was the girl of last night. He saw no resemblance to Minna at all.

"I'll run you home," he said. "Where do you live?"

"Run me home?" She was startled. "There's no hurry – I'm sorry if I offended you."

"No. It was nice of you to come. I've been stupid. Last night I had an idea that you were an exact double for someone I knew. It was dark and the light was in my eyes."

She was offended – he had reproached her for not looking like someone else.

"It was just that!" she said. "That's funny."

They rode in silence for a minute.

"You were married to Minna Davis, weren't you?" she said with a flash of intuition. "Excuse me for referring to it."

He was driving as fast as he could without making it conspicuous.

"I'm quite a different type from Minna Davis," she said. "If that's who you meant. You might have referred to the girl who was with me. She looks more like Minna Davis than I do."

That was of no interest now. The thing was to get this over quick and forget it.

"Could it have been her?" she asked. "She lives next door."

"Not possibly," he said. "I remember the silver belt you wore."

"That was me all right."

They were north-west of Sunset, climbing one of the canyons through the hills. Lighted bungalows rose along the winding road, and the electric current that animated them sweated into the evening air as radio sound.

"You see that last highest light – Kathleen lives there. I live just over the top of the hill."

A moment later she said, "Stop here."

"I thought you said over the top."

"I want to stop at Kathleen's."

"I'm afraid I'm—"

"I want to get out here myself," she said impatiently.

Stahr slid out after her. She started towards a new little house almost roofed over by a single willow tree, and automatically he followed her to the steps. She rang a bell and turned to say goodnight.

"I'm sorry you were disappointed," she said.

He was sorry for her now – sorry for them both.

"It was my fault. Goodnight."

A wedge of light came out the opening door, and as a girl's voice enquired "Who is it?" Stahr looked up.

There she was – face and form and smile against the light from inside. It was Minna's face – the skin with its peculiar radiance as if phosphorus had touched it, the mouth with its warm line that never counted costs – and over all the haunting jollity that had fascinated a generation.

With a leap his heart went out of him as it had the night before, only this time it stayed out there with a vast beneficence.

"Oh, Edna, you can't come in," the girl said. "I've been cleaning and the house is full of ammonia smell."

Edna began to laugh, bold and loud. "I believe it was you he wanted to see, Kathleen," she said.

Stahr's eyes and Kathleen's met and tangled. For an instant they made love as no one ever dares to do after. Their glance was slower than an embrace, more urgent than a call.

"He telephoned me," said Edna. "It seems he thought—"

Stahr interrupted, stepping forward into the light.

"I was afraid we were rude at the studio, yesterday evening."

But there were no words for what he really said. She listened closely without shame. Life flared high in them both – Edna seemed at a distance and in darkness.

"You weren't rude," said Kathleen. A cool wind blew the brown curls around her forehead. "We had no business there."

"I hope you'll both," Stahr said, "come and make a tour of the studio."

"Who are you? Somebody important?"

"He was Minna Davis's husband, he's a producer," said Edna, as if it were a rare joke. "And this isn't at all what he just told me. I think he has a crush on you."

"Shut up, Edna," said Kathleen sharply.

As if suddenly realizing her offensiveness, Edna said, "Phone me, will you?" and stalked away towards the road. But she carried their secret with her – she had seen a spark pass between them in the darkness.

"I remember you," Kathleen said to Stahr. "You got us out of the flood."

Now what? The other woman was more missed in her absence. They were alone and on too slim a basis for what had passed already. They existed nowhere. His world seemed far away – she had no world at all except the idol's head, the half-open door.

"You're Irish," he said, trying to build one for her.

She nodded.

"I've lived in London a long time – I didn't think you could tell."

The wild green eyes of a bus sped up the road in the darkness. They were silent until it went by.

"Your friend Edna didn't like me," he said. "I think it was the word Producer."

"She's just come out here too. She's a silly creature who means no harm. *I* shouldn't be afraid of you."

She searched his face. She thought, like everyone, that he seemed tired – then she forgot it at the impression he gave of a brazier out of doors on a cool night.

"I suppose the girls are all after you to put them on the screen."

"They've given up," he said.

This was an understatement – they were all there, he knew, just over the threshold, but they had been there so long that their clamouring voices were no more than the sound of the traffic in the street. But his position remained more than royal: a king could make only one queen; Stahr, at least so they supposed, could make many.

"I'm thinking that it would turn you into a cynic," she said. "You didn't want to put me in pictures?"

"No."

"That's good. I'm no actress. Once in London a man came up to me in the Carlton and asked me to make a test, but I thought a while and finally I didn't go."

They had been standing nearly motionless, as if in a moment he would leave and she would go in. Stahr laughed suddenly.

"I feel as if I had my foot in the door – like a collector."

She laughed too.

"I'm sorry I can't ask you in. Shall I get my reefer and sit outside?"

"No." He scarcely knew why he felt it was time to go. He might see her again – he might not. It was just as well this way.

"You'll come to the studio?" he said. "I can't promise to go around with you, but if you come, you must be sure to send word to my office."

A frown, the shadow of a hair in breadth, appeared between her eyes.

"I'm not sure," she said. "But I'm very much obliged."

He knew that, for some reason, she would not come – in an instant she had slipped away from him. They both sensed that the moment was played out. He must go, even though he went nowhere, and it left him with nothing. Practically, vulgarly, he did not have her telephone number – or even her name – but it seemed impossible to ask for them now.

She walked with him to the car, her glowing beauty and her unexplored novelty pressing up against him, but there was a foot of moonlight between them when they came out of the shadow.

"Is this all?" he said spontaneously.

He saw regret in her face – but there was a flick of the lip also, a bending of the smile towards some indirection, a momentary dropping and lifting of a curtain over a forbidden passage.

"I do hope we'll meet again," she said almost formally.

"I'd be sorry if we didn't."

They were distant for a moment. But as he turned his car in the next drive, and came back with her still waiting, and waved and drove on, he felt exalted and happy. He was glad that there was beauty in the world that would not be weighed in the scales of the casting department.

But at home he felt a curious loneliness as his butler made him tea in the samovar. It was the old hurt come back, heavy and delightful. When he took up the first of two scripts that were his evening stint, that presently he would visualize line by line on the screen, he waited a moment, thinking of Minna. He explained to her that it was really nothing, that no one could ever be like she was, that he was sorry.

* * *

That was substantially a day of Stahr's. I don't know about the illness, when it started, etc., because he was secretive, but I know he fainted a couple of times that month, because Father told me. Prince Agge is my authority for the luncheon in the commissary where he told them he was going to make a picture that would lose money – which was something, considering the men he had to deal with and that he held a big block of stock and had a profit-sharing contract.

And Wylie White told me a lot, which I believed, because he felt Stahr intensely with a mixture of jealousy and admiration. As for me, I was head over heels in love with him then, and you can take what I say for what it's worth.

Chapter 5

F RESH AS THE MORNING, I went up to see him a week
later. Or so I thought: when Wylie called for me, I had
gotten into riding clothes to give the impression I'd been out
in the dew since early morning.

"I'm going to throw myself under the wheel of Stahr's car
this morning," I said.

"How about this car?" he suggested. "It's one of the best
cars Mort Fleishacker ever sold second-hand."

"Not on your flowing veil," I answered like a book. "You
have a wife in the East."

"She's the past," he said. "You've got one great card, Celia –
your valuation of yourself. Do you think anybody would look
at you if you weren't Pat Brady's daughter?"

We don't take abuse like our mothers would have. Nothing
– no remark from a contemporary means much. They tell you
to be smart, they're marrying you for your money, or you tell
them. Everything's simpler. Or is it? – as we used to say.

But as I turned on the radio and the car raced up Laurel
Canyon to 'The Thundering Beat of My Heart',* I didn't
believe he was right. I had good features, except my face was
too round, and a skin they seemed to love to touch, and good
legs, and I didn't have to wear a brassiere. I haven't a sweet
nature, but who was Wylie to reproach me for that?

"Don't you think I'm smart to go in the morning?" I asked.

"Yeah. To the busiest man in California. He'll appreciate it. Why didn't you wake him up at four?"

"That's just it. At night he's tired. He's been looking at people all day, and some of them not bad. I come in in the morning and start a train of thought."

"I don't like it. It's brazen."

"What have you got to offer? And don't be rough."

"I love you," he said without much conviction. "I love you more than I love your money, and that's plenty. Maybe your father would make me a supervisor."

"I could marry the last man tapped for Bones* this year and live in Southampton."

I turned the dial and got either 'Gone' or 'Lost' – there were good songs that year. The music was getting better again. When I was young during the Depression, it wasn't so hot, and the best numbers were from the Twenties, like Benny Goodman playing 'Blue Heaven'* or Paul Whiteman with 'When Day Is Done'.* There were only the bands to listen to. But now I liked almost everything except Father singing 'Little Girl, You've Had a Busy Day'* to try to create a sentimental father-and-daughter feeling.

'Lost' and 'Gone' were the wrong mood, so I turned again and got 'Lovely to Look at',* which was my kind of poetry. I looked back as we crossed the crest of the foothills – with the air so clear you could see the leaves on Sunset Mountain two miles away. It's startling to you sometimes – just air, unobstructed, uncomplicated air.

"*Lovely to look at – de-lightful to know-w*," I sang.

"Are you going to sing for Stahr?" Wylie said. "If you do, get in a line about my being a good supervisor."

"Oh, this'll be only Stahr and me," I said. "He's going to look at me and think, 'I've never really seen her before.'"

"We don't use that line this year," he said.

"Then he'll say 'Little Cecilia', like he did the night of the earthquake. He'll say he never noticed I have become a woman."

"You won't have to do a thing."

"I'll stand there and bloom. After he kisses me as you would a child—"

"That's all in my script," complained Wylie, "and I've got to show it to him tomorrow."

"—he'll sit down and put his face in his hands and say he never thought of me like that."

"You mean you get in a little fast work during the kiss?"

"I bloom, I told you. How often do I have to tell you I bloom."

"It's beginning to sound pretty randy to me," said Wylie. "How about laying off – I've got to work this morning."

"Then he says it seems as if he was always meant to be this way."

"Right in the industry. Producer's blood." He pretended to shiver. "I'd hate to have a transfusion of that."

"Then he says—"

"I know all his lines," said Wylie. "What I want to know is what you say."

"Somebody comes in," I went on.

"And you jump up quickly off the casting couch, smoothing your skirts."

"Do you want me to walk out and get home?"

We were in Beverly Hills, getting very beautiful now with the tall Hawaiian pines. Hollywood is a perfectly zoned city, so you know exactly what kind of people economically live in each section, from executives and directors, through technicians in their bungalows, right down to extras. This was the executive section and a very fancy lot of pastry. It wasn't as romantic as the dingiest village of Virginia or New Hampshire, but it looked nice this morning.

"*They asked me how I knew*," sang the radio, "*my true love was true.*"*

My heart was fire, and smoke was in my eyes and everything, but I figured my chance at about fifty-fifty. I would walk right up on him as if I was either going to walk through him or kiss him on the mouth – and stop a bare foot away and say "Hello" with disarming understatement.

And I did – though of course it wasn't like I expected: Stahr's beautiful dark eyes looking back into mine, knowing, I am dead sure, everything I was thinking – and not a bit embarrassed. I stood there an hour, I think, without moving, and all he did was twitch the side of his mouth and put his hands in his pockets.

"Will you go with me to the ball tonight?" I asked.

"What ball?"

"The screenwriters' ball down at the Ambassador."

"Oh, yes." He considered. "I can't go with you. I might just come in late. We've got a sneak preview in Glendale."

How different it all was from what you'd planned. When he sat down, I went over and put my head among his telephones, like a sort of desk appendage, and looked at him; and his dark eyes looked back so kind and nothing. Men don't often know those times when a girl could be had for nothing. All I succeeded in putting into his head was:

"Why don't you get married, Celia?"

Maybe he'd bring up Robby again, try to make a match there. "What could I do to interest an interesting man?" I asked him.

"Tell him you're in love with him."

"Should I chase him?"

"Yes," he said smiling.

"I don't know. If it isn't there, it isn't there."

"I'd marry you," he said unexpectedly. "I'm lonesome as hell. But I'm too old and tired to undertake anything."

I went around the desk and stood beside him.

"Undertake me."

He looked up in surprise, understanding for the first time that I was in deadly earnest.

"Oh, no," he said. He looked almost miserable for a minute. "Pictures are my girl. I haven't got much time…" He corrected himself quickly, "I mean any time."

"You couldn't love me."

"It's not that," he said and – right out of my dream but with a difference: "I never thought of you that way, Celia. I've known you so long. Somebody told me you were going to marry Wylie White."

"And you had… no reaction."

"Yes, I did. I was going to speak to you about it. Wait till he's been sober for two years."

"I'm not even considering it, Monroe."

We were way off the track, and just as in my daydream, somebody came in – only I was quite sure Stahr had pressed a concealed button.

I'll always think of that moment, when I felt Miss Doolan behind me with her pad, as the end of childhood, the end of the time when you cut out pictures. What I was looking at wasn't Stahr, but a picture of him I cut out over and over: the eyes that flashed a sophisticated understanding at you and then darted up too soon into his wide brow with its ten thousand plots and plans; the face that was ageing from within, so that there were no casual furrows of worry and vexation but a drawn asceticism as if from a silent self-set struggle – or a long illness. It was handsomer to me than all the rosy tan from Coronado to Del Monte. He was my picture, as sure as if he had been pasted on the inside of my old locker in school. That's what I told Wylie White, and when a girl tells the man she likes second best about the other one – then she's in love.

* * *

I noticed the girl long before Stahr arrived at the dance. Not a pretty girl, for there are none of those in Los Angeles – one girl can be pretty, but a dozen are only a chorus. Nor yet a professional beauty – they do all the breathing for everyone, and finally even the men have to go outside for air. Just a girl, with the skin of one of Raphael's corner angels and a style that made you look back twice to see if it were something she had on.

I noticed her and forgot her. She was sitting back behind the pillars at a table whose ornament was a faded semi-star who, in hopes of being noticed and getting a bit, rose and danced regularly with some scarecrow males. It reminded me shamefully of my first party, where Mother made me dance over and over with the same boy to keep in the spotlight. The semi-star spoke to several people at our table, but we were busy being Café Society and she got nowhere at all.

From our angle it appeared that they all wanted something.

"You're expected to fling it around," said Wylie, "like in the old days. When they find out you're hanging on to it, they get discouraged. That's what all this brave gloom is about – the only way to keep their self-respect is to be Hemingway characters. But underneath they hate you in a mournful way, and you know it."

He was right – I knew that since 1933 the rich could only be happy alone together.

I saw Stahr come into the half-light at the top of the wide steps and stand there with his hands in his pockets, looking around. It was late and the lights seemed to have burnt a little lower, though they were the same. The floor show was finished, except for a man who still wore a placard which said that at midnight in the Hollywood Bowl Sonja Henie* was going to skate on hot soup. You could see the sign as he danced becoming less funny on his back. A few years before there would have been drunks around. The faded actress seemed to be looking for them hopefully over her partner's shoulder. I followed her with my eyes when she went back to her table…

…and there, to my surprise, was Stahr talking to the other girl. They were smiling at each other as if this was the beginning of the world.

* * *

Stahr had expected nothing like this when he stood at the head of the steps a few minutes earlier. The "sneak preview" had disappointed him, and afterwards he had had a scene with Jacques La Borwitz right in front of the theatre, for which he was now sorry. He had started towards the Brady party, when he saw Kathleen sitting in the middle of a long white table alone.

Immediately things changed. As he walked towards her, the people shrank back against the walls till they were only murals; the white table lengthened and became an altar where the priestess sat alone. Vitality swelled up in him, and he could have stood a long time across the table from her, looking and smiling.

The incumbents of the table were crawling back – Stahr and Kathleen danced.

When she came close, his several visions of her blurred; she was momentarily unreal. Usually a girl's skull made her real, but not this time – Stahr continued to be dazzled as they danced out along the floor – to the last edge, where they stepped through a mirror into another dance with new dancers whose faces were familiar but nothing more. In this new region he talked, fast and urgently.

"What's your name?"

"Kathleen Moore."

"Kathleen Moore," he repeated.

"I have no telephone, if that's what you're thinking."

"When will you come to the studio?"

"It's not possible. Truly."

"Why isn't it? Are you married?"

"No."

"You're not married?"

"No, nor never have been. But then I may be."

"Someone there at the table."

"No." She laughed. "What curiosity!"

But she was deep in it with him, no matter what the words were. Her eyes invited him to a romantic communion of unbelievable intensity. As if she realized this, she said, frightened:

"I must go back now. I promised this dance."

"I don't want to lose you. Couldn't we have lunch or dinner?"

"It's impossible." But her expression helplessly amended the words to: "It's just possible. The door is still open by a chink, if you could squeeze past. But quickly – so little time."

"I must go back," she repeated aloud. Then she dropped her arms, stopped dancing and looked at him, a laughing wanton.

"When I'm with you, I don't breathe quite right," she said.

She turned, picked up her long dress and stepped back through the mirror. Stahr followed until she stopped near her table.

"Thank you for the dance," she said, "and now, really, goodnight."

Then she nearly ran.

Stahr went to the table where he was expected and sat down with the Café Society group – from Wall Street, Grand Street, Loudon County, Virginia, and Odessa, Russia. They were all talking with enthusiasm about a horse that had run very fast, and Mr Marcus was the most enthusiastic of all. Stahr guessed that the Jews had taken over the worship of horses as a symbol – for years it had been the Cossacks mounted and the Jews on foot. Now the Jews had horses, and it gave them a sense of extraordinary well-being and power. Stahr sat pretending to listen and even nodding when something was referred to him, but all the time watching the table behind the pillars. If everything had not happened as it had, even to his connecting the silver belt with the wrong girl, he might have thought it was some elaborate frame-up. But the elusiveness was beyond suspicion. For there in a moment he saw that she was escaping again – the pantomime at the table indicated goodbye. She was leaving, she was gone.

"There," said Wylie White with malice, "goes Cinderella. Simply bring the slipper to the Regal Shoe Company, 812 South Broadway."

Stahr overtook her in the long upper lobby, where middle-aged women sat behind a roped-off space, watching the ball-room entrance.

"Am I responsible for this?" he asked.

"I was going, anyhow." But she added, almost resentfully, "They talked as if I'd been dancing with the Prince of Wales. They all stared at me. One of the men wanted to draw my picture, and another one wanted to see me tomorrow."

"That's just what I want," said Stahr gently, "but I want to see you much more than he does."

"You insist so," she said wearily. "One reason I left England was that men always wanted their own way. I thought it was different here. Isn't it enough that I don't want to see you?"

"Ordinarily," agreed Stahr. "Please believe me, I'm way out of my depth already. I feel like a fool. But I must see you again and talk to you."

She hesitated.

"There's no reason for feeling like a fool," she said. "You're too good a man to feel like a fool. But you should see this for what it is."

"What is it?"

"You've fallen for me – completely. You've got me in your dreams."

"I'd forgotten you," he declared, "till the moment I walked in that door."

"Forgotten me with your head perhaps. But I knew the first time I saw you that you were the kind that likes me..."

She stopped herself. Near them a man and woman from the party were saying goodbye: "Tell her hello – tell her I love her dearly," said the woman. "You both – all of you – the children." Stahr could not talk like that, the way everyone talked now. He could think of nothing further to say as they walked towards the elevator except:

"I suppose you're perfectly right."

"Oh, you admit it?"

"No, I don't," he retracted. "It's just the whole way you're made. What you say – how you walk – the way you look right this minute..." He saw she had melted a little, and his hopes rose. "Tomorrow is Sunday, and usually I work on Sunday, but if there's anything you're curious about in Hollywood, any person you want to meet or see, please let me arrange it."

They were standing by the elevator. It opened, but she let it go.

"You're very modest," she said. "You always talk about showing me the studio and taking me around. Don't you ever stay alone?"

"Tomorrow I'll feel very much alone."

"Oh, the poor man – I could weep for him. He could have all the stars jumping around him and he chooses me."

He smiled – he had laid himself open to that one.

The elevator came again. She signalled for it to wait.

"I'm a weak woman," she said. "If I meet you tomorrow, will you leave me in peace? No, you won't. You'll make it worse. It wouldn't do any good, but harm, so I'll say no and thank you."

She got into the elevator. Stahr got in too, and they smiled as they dropped two floors to the hall, cross-sectioned with small shops. Down at the end, held back by police, was the crowd, their heads and shoulders leaning forward to look down the alley. Kathleen shivered.

"They looked so strange when I came in," she said, "as if they were furious at me for not being someone famous."

"I know another way out," said Stahr.

They went through a drugstore, down an alley, and came out into the clear cool California night beside the car park. He felt detached from the dance now, and she did too.

"A lot of picture people used to live down here," he said. "John Barrymore and Pola Negri* in those bungalows. And Connie Talmadge* lived in that tall thin apartment house over the way."

"Doesn't anybody live here now?"

"The studios moved out into the country," he said. "What used to be the country. I had some good times around here, though."

He did not mention that ten years ago Minna and her mother had lived in another apartment over the way.

"How old are you?" she asked suddenly.

"I've lost track – almost thirty-five, I think."

"They said at the table you were the boy wonder."

"I'll be that when I'm sixty," he said grimly. "You will meet me tomorrow, won't you?"

"I'll meet you," she said. "Where?"

Suddenly there was no place to meet. She would not go to a party at anyone's house, nor to the country, nor swimming, though she hesitated, nor to a well-known restaurant. She seemed hard to please, but he knew there was some reason. He would find out in time. It occurred to him that she might be the sister or daughter of someone well-known who was pledged to keep in the background. He suggested that he come for her and they could decide.

"That wouldn't do," she said. "What about right here? The same spot."

He nodded – pointing up at the arch under which they stood.

He put her into her car, which would have brought eighty dollars from any kindly dealer, and watched it rasp away. Down by the entrance a cheer went up as a favourite emerged, and Stahr wondered whether to show himself and say goodnight.

* * *

This is Celia taking up the narrative in person. Stahr came back finally – it was about half-past three – and asked me to dance.

"How are you?" he asked me, just as if he hadn't seen me that morning. "I got involved in a long conversation with a man."

It was secret too – he cared that much about it.

"I took him for a drive," he went on innocently. "I didn't realize how much this part of Hollywood had changed."

"Has it changed?"

"Oh, yes," he said, "changed completely. Unrecognizable. I couldn't tell you exactly, but it's all changed – everything. It's like a new city." After a moment he amplified: "I had no idea how much it had changed."

"Who was the man?" I ventured.

"An old friend," he said vaguely, "someone I knew a long time ago."

I had made Wylie try to find out quietly who she was. He had gone over and the ex-star had asked him excitedly to sit down. No: she didn't know who the girl was – a friend of a friend of someone – even the man who had brought her didn't know.

So Stahr and I danced to the beautiful music of Glenn Miller playing 'I'm on a See-Saw'.* It was good dancing now, with plenty of room. But it was lonely – lonelier than before the girl had gone. For me, as well as for Stahr, she took the evening with her, took along the stabbing pain I had felt – left the great ballroom empty and without emotion. Now it was nothing, and I was dancing with an absent-minded man who told me how much Los Angeles had changed.

* * *

They met, next afternoon, as strangers in an unfamiliar country. Last night was gone, the girl he had danced with was gone. A misty rose-and-blue hat with a trifling veil came along the terrace to him and paused, searching his face. Stahr was strange too, in a brown suit and a black tie that blocked him out more tangibly than a formal dinner coat, or when he was simply a face and voice in the darkness the night they had first met.

He was the first to be sure it was the same person as before: the upper part of the face that was Minna's, luminous, with creamy temples and opalescent brown – the cool-coloured curly hair. He could have put his arm around her and pulled her close with an almost family familiarity – already he knew the down on her neck, the very set of her backbone, the corners of her eyes and how she breathed – the very texture of the clothes that she would wear.

"Did you wait here all night?" she said, in a voice that was like a whisper.

"I didn't move – didn't stir."

Still the problem remained, the same one – there was no special place to go.

"I'd like tea," she suggested, "if it's some place you're not known."

"That sounds as if one of us had a bad reputation."

"Doesn't it?" she laughed.

"We'll go to the shore," Stahr suggested. "There's a place there where I got out once and was chased by a trained seal."

"Do you think the seal could make tea?"

"Well – he's trained. And I don't think he'll talk – I don't think his training got that far. What in *hell* are you trying to hide?"

After a moment she said lightly: "Perhaps the future," in a way that might mean anything or nothing at all.

As they drove away, she pointed at her jalopy in the parking lot.

"Do you think it's safe?"

"I doubt it. I noticed some black-bearded foreigners snooping around."

Kathleen looked at him alarmed.

"Really?" She saw he was smiling. "I believe everything you say," she said. "You've got such a gentle way about you that I don't see why they're all so afraid of you." She examined him with approval – fretting a little about his pallor, which was accentuated by the bright afternoon. "Do you work very hard? Do you really always work on Sundays?"

He responded to her interest – impersonal yet not perfunctory.

"Not always. Once we had… we had a house with a pool and all – and people came on Sunday. I played tennis and swam. I don't swim any more."

"Why not? It's good for you. I thought all Americans swam."

"My legs got very thin – a few years ago, and it embarrassed me. There were other things I used to do – lots of things: I used to play handball when I was a kid, and sometimes out here – I had a court that was washed away in a storm."

"You have a good build," she said in formal compliment, meaning only that he was made with thin grace.

He rejected this with a shake of his head.

"I enjoy working most," he said. "My work is very congenial."

"Did you always want to be in movies?"

"No. When I was young I wanted to be a chief clerk – the one who knew where everything was."

She smiled.

"That's odd. And now you're much more than that."

"No, I'm still a chief clerk," Stahr said. "That's my gift, if I have one. Only when I got to be it, I found out that no one knew where anything was. And I found out that you had to know why it was where it was, and whether it should be left there. They began throwing it all at me, and it was a very complex office. Pretty soon I had all the keys. And they wouldn't have remembered what locks they fitted if I'd given them back."

They stopped for a red light, and a newsboy bleated at him: "Mickey Mouse Murdered! Randolph Hearst* declares war on China!"

"We'll have to buy this paper," she said.

As they drove on, she straightened her hat and preened herself. Seeing him looking at her, she smiled.

She was alert and calm – qualities that were currently at a premium. There was lassitude in plenty – California was filling up with weary desperados. And there were tense young men and women who lived back East in spirit while they carried on a losing battle against the climate. But it was everyone's secret that sustained effort was difficult here – a secret that Stahr scarcely admitted to himself. But he knew that people from other places spurted a pure rill of new energy for a while.

They were very friendly now. She had not made a move or a gesture that was out of keeping with her beauty, that pressed it out of its contour one way or another. It was all proper to itself. He judged her as he would a shot in a picture. She was not trash, she was not confused, but clear – in his special meaning of the word, which implied balance, delicacy and proportion – she was "nice".

They reached Santa Monica, where there were the stately houses of a dozen picture stars, penned in the middle of a crawling Coney Island. They turned downhill into the wide blue sky and sea and went on along the sea till the beach slid out again from under the bathers in a widening and narrowing yellow strand.

"I'm building a house out here," Stahr said, "much farther on. I don't know why I'm building it."

"Perhaps it's for me," she said.

"Maybe it is."

"I think it's splendid for you to build a big house for me without even knowing what I looked like."

"It isn't too big. And it hasn't any roof. I didn't know what kind of roof you wanted."

"We don't want a roof. They told me it never rained here. It…"

She stopped so suddenly that he knew she was reminded of something.

"Just something that's past," she said.

"What was it?" he demanded. "Another house without a roof?"

"Yes. Another house without a roof."

"Were you happy there?"

"I lived with a man," she said, "a long, long time – too long. It was one of those awful mistakes people make. I lived with him a long time after I wanted to get out, but he couldn't let me go. He'd try, but he couldn't. So finally I ran away."

He was listening, weighing but not judging. Nothing changed under the rose and blue hat. She was twenty-five or so. It would have been a waste if she had not loved and been loved.

"We were too close," she said. "We should probably have had children – to stand between us. But you can't have children when there's no roof to the house."

All right, he knew something of her. It would not be like last night when something kept saying, as in a story conference: "We know nothing about the girl. We don't have to know much – but we have to know something." A vague background spread behind her, something more tangible than the head of Shiva in the moonlight.

They came to the restaurant, forbidding with many Sunday automobiles. When they got out, the trained seal growled reminiscently at Stahr. The man who owned it said that the seal would never ride in the back seat of his car but always climbed over the back and up in front. It was plain that the man was in bondage to the seal, though he had not yet acknowledged it to himself.

"I'd like to see the house you're building," said Kathleen. "I don't want tea – tea is the past."

Kathleen drank a Coke instead and they drove on ten miles into a sun so bright that he took out two pairs of cheaters from a compartment. Five miles farther on they turned down a small promontory and came to the fuselage of Stahr's house.

A headwind blowing out of the sun threw spray up the rocks and over the car. Concrete mixer, raw yellow wood and builders' rubble waited, an open wound in the seascape for Sunday to be over. They walked around front, where great boulders rose to what would be the terrace.

She looked at the feeble hills behind and winced faintly at the barren glitter, and Stahr saw...

"No use looking for what's not here," he said cheerfully. "Think of it as if you were standing on one of those globes with a map on it – I always wanted one when I was a boy."

"I understand," she said after a minute. "When you do that, you can feel the earth turn, can't you?"

He nodded.

"Yes. Otherwise it's all just *mañana* – waiting for the morning or the moon."

They went in under the scaffolding. One room, which was to be the chief salon, was completed even to the built-in bookshelves and the curtain rods and the trap in the floor for the motion-picture projection machine. And to her surprise, this opened out to a porch with cushioned chairs in place and a ping-pong table. There was another ping-pong table on the newly laid sod beyond.

"Last week I gave a premature luncheon," he admitted, "I had some props brought out – some grass and things. I wanted to see how the place felt."

She laughed suddenly.

"Isn't that real grass?"

"Oh yes – it's grass."

Beyond the strip of anticipatory lawn was the excavation for a swimming pool, patronized now by a crowd of seagulls, which saw them and took flight.

"Are you going to live here all alone?" she asked him. "Not even dancing girls?"

"Probably. I used to make plans, but not any more. I thought this would be a nice place to read scripts. The studio is really home."

"That's what I've heard about American businessmen."

He caught a tilt of criticism in her voice.

"You do what you're born to do," he said gently. "About once a month somebody tries to reform me, tells me what a barren old age I'll have when I can't work any more. But it's not so simple."

The wind was rising. It was time to go, and he had his car keys out of his pocket, absent-mindedly jingling them in his hand. There was the silvery "Hey!" of a telephone, coming from somewhere across the sunshine.

It was not from the house, and they hurried here and there around the garden, like children playing warmer and colder – closing in finally on a tool shack by the tennis court. The phone, irked with delay, barked at them suspiciously from the wall. Stahr hesitated.

"Shall I let the damn thing ring?"

"I couldn't. Unless I was sure who it was."

"Either it's for somebody else or they've made a wild guess."

He picked up the receiver.

"Hello... Long distance from where? Yes, this is Mr Stahr."

His manner changed perceptibly. She saw what few people had seen for a decade: Stahr impressed. It was not discordant, because he often pretended to be impressed, but it made him momentarily a little younger.

"It's the President," he said to her, almost stiffly.

"Of your company?"

"No, of the United States."

He was trying to be casual for her benefit, but his voice was eager.

"All right, I'll wait," he said into the phone, and then to Kathleen: "I've talked to him before."

She watched. He smiled at her and winked, as an evidence that while he must give this his best attention, he had not forgotten her.

"Hello," he said presently. He listened. Then he said "Hello" again. He frowned.

"Can you talk a little louder," he said politely, and then: "Who?... What's that?"

She saw a disgusted look come into his face.

"I don't want to talk to him," he said. "No!"

He turned to Kathleen:

"Believe it or not, it's an orang-utan."

He waited while something was explained to him at length; then he repeated:

"I don't want to talk to it, Lew. I haven't got anything to say that would interest an orang-utan."

He beckoned to Kathleen, and when she came close to the phone he held the receiver so that she heard odd breathing and a gruff growl. Then a voice:

"This is no phoney, Monroe. It can talk and it's a dead ringer for McKinley.* Mr Horace Wickersham is with me here with a picture of McKinley in his hand..."

Stahr listened patiently.

"We've got a chimp," he said, after a minute. "He bit a chunk out of John Gilbert* last year... All right, put him on again."

He spoke formally, as if to a child.

"Hello, orang-utan."

His face changed, and he turned to Kathleen.

"He said 'Hello'."

"Ask him his name," suggested Kathleen.

"Hello, orang-utan – God, what a thing to be! – do you know your name?... He doesn't seem to know his name.... Listen, Lew. We're not making anything like *King Kong*, and there is no monkey in *The Hairy Ape*...* Of course I'm sure. I'm sorry, Lew, goodbye."

He was annoyed with Lew, because he had thought it was the President and had changed his manner, acting as if it were. He felt a little ridiculous, but Kathleen felt sorry and liked him better because it had been an orang-utan.

* * *

They started back along the shore with the sun behind them. The house seemed kindlier when they left it, as if warmed by their visit – the hard glitter of the place was more endurable if they were not bound there like people on the shiny surface of a moon. Looking back from a curve of the shore, they saw the sky growing pink behind the indecisive structure, and the point of land seemed a friendly island, not without promise of fine hours on a further day.

Past Malibu, with its gaudy shacks and fishing barges, they came into the range of humankind again, the cars stacked and piled along the road, the beaches like anthills without a pattern, save for the dark drowned heads that sprinkled the sea.

Goods from the city were increasing in sight – blankets, matting, umbrellas, cook stoves, reticules full of clothing – the prisoners had laid out their shackles beside them on this sand. It was Stahr's sea if he wanted it, or knew what to do with it – only by sufferance did these others wet their feet and fingers in the wild cool reservoirs of man's world.

Stahr turned off the road by the sea and up a canyon and along a hill road, and the people dropped away. The hill became the outskirts of the city. Stopping for gasoline, he stood beside the car.

"We could have dinner," he said almost anxiously.

"You have work you could do."

"No – I haven't planned anything. Couldn't we have dinner?"

He knew that she had nothing to do either – no planned evening or special place to go.

She compromised.

"Do you want to get something in that drugstore across the street?"

He looked at it tentatively.

"Is that really what you want?"

"I like to eat in American drugstores. It seems so queer and strange."

They sat on high stools and had tomato broth and hot sand-wiches. It was more intimate than anything they had done, and they both felt a dangerous sort of loneliness, and felt it in each other. They shared in varied scents of the drugstore, bitter and sweet and sour, and the mystery of the waitress, with only the outer part of her hair dyed and black beneath, and, when it was over, the still life of their empty plates – a sliver of potato, a sliced pickle and an olive stone.

* * *

It was dusk in the street, it seemed nothing to smile at him now when they got into the car.

"Thank you so much. It's been a nice afternoon."

It was not far from her house. They felt the beginning of the hill, and the louder sound of the car in second was the begin-ning of the end. Lights were on in the climbing bungalows – he turned on the headlights of the car. Stahr felt heavy in the pit of his stomach.

"We'll go out again."

"No," she said quickly, as if she had been expecting this. "I'll write you a letter. I'm sorry I've been so mysterious – it was really a compliment, because I like you so much. You should try not to work so hard. You ought to marry again."

"Oh, that isn't what you should say," he broke out protestingly. "This has been you and me today. It may have meant nothing to you – it meant a lot to me. I'd like time to tell you about it."

But if he were to take time it must be in her house, for they were there and she was shaking her head as the car drew up to the door.

"I must go now. I do have an engagement. I didn't tell you."

"That's not true. But it's all right."

He walked to the door with her and stood in his own foot-steps of that other night, while she felt in her bag for the key.

"Have you got it?"

"I've got it," she said.

That was the moment to go in, but she wanted to see him once more and she leant her head to the left, then to the right, trying to catch his face against the last twilight. She leant too far and too long, and it was natural when his hand touched the back of her upper arm and shoulder and pressed her forward into the darkness of his throat. She shut her eyes, feeling the bevel of the key in her tight-clutched hand. She said "Oh" in an expiring sigh, and then "Oh" again, as he pulled her in close and his chin pushed her cheek around gently. They were both smiling just faintly, and she was frowning too, as the inch between them melted into darkness.

When they were apart, she shook her head still, but more in wonder than in denial. It came like this then, it was your own fault, now far back, when was the moment? It came like this, and every instant the burden of tearing herself away from them together, from it, was heavier and more unimaginable. He was exultant; she resented and could not blame him, but she would not be part of his exultation, for it was a defeat. So far it was a defeat. And then she thought that if she stopped it being a defeat, broke off and went inside, it was still not a victory. Then it was just nothing.

"This was not my idea," she said, "not at all my idea."

"Can I come in?"

"Oh, no – no."

"Then let's jump in the car and drive somewhere."

With relief, she caught at the exact phrasing – to get away from here immediately, that was accomplishment or sounded like it – as if she were fleeing from the spot of a crime. Then they were in the car, going downhill with the breeze cool in their faces, and she came slowly to herself. Now it was all clear in black and white.

"We'll go back to your house on the beach," she said.

"Back there?"

"Yes – we'll go back to your house. Don't let's talk. I just want to ride."

* * *

When they got to the coast again the sky was grey, and at Santa Monica a sudden gust of rain bounced over them. Stahr halted beside the road, put on a raincoat and lifted the canvas top. "We've got a roof," he said.

The windshield wiper ticked domestically as a grandfather's clock. Sullen cars were leaving the wet beaches and starting back into the city. Farther on they ran into fog – the road lost its boundaries on either side, and the lights of cars coming towards them were stationary until just before they flared past.

They had left a part of themselves behind, and they felt light and free in the car. Fog fizzed in at a chink, and Kathleen took off the rose-and-blue hat in a calm, slow way that made him watch tensely, and put it under a strip of canvas in the back seat. She shook out her hair and, when she saw Stahr was looking at her, she smiled.

The trained seal's restaurant was only a sheen of light off towards the ocean. Stahr cranked down a window and looked for landmarks, but after a few more miles the fog fell away, and just ahead of them the road turned off that led to his house. Out here a moon showed behind the clouds. There was still a shifting light over the sea.

The house had dissolved a little back into its elements. They found the dripping beams of a doorway and groped over mysterious waist-high obstacles to the single finished room, odorous of sawdust and wet wood. When he took her in his arms, they could just see each other's eyes in the half-darkness. Presently his raincoat dropped to the floor.

"Wait," she said.

She needed a minute. She did not see how any good could come from this, and though this did not prevent her from being happy and desirous, she needed a minute to think how it was, to go back an hour and know how it had happened. She waited in his arms, moving her head a little from side to side as she had before, only more slowly, and never taking her eyes from his. Then she discovered that he was trembling.

He discovered it at the same time, and his arms relaxed. Immediately she spoke to him coarsely and provocatively, and pulled his face down to hers. Then, with her knees she struggled out of something, still standing up and holding him with one arm, and kicked it off beside the coat. He was not trembling now and he held her again, as they knelt down together and slid to the raincoat on the floor.

* * *

Afterwards they lay without speaking, and then he was full of such tender love for her that he held her tight till a stitch tore in her dress. The small sound brought them to reality.

"I'll help you up," he said, taking her hands.

"Not just yet. I was thinking of something."

She lay in the darkness, thinking irrationally that it would be such a bright indefatigable baby, but presently she let him help her up... When she came back into the room, it was lit from a single electric fixture.

"A one-bulb lighting system," he said. "Shall I turn it off?"

"No. It's very nice. I want to see you."

They sat in the wooden frame of the window seat, with the soles of their shoes touching.

"You seem far away," she said.

"So do you."

"Are you surprised?"

"At what?"

"That we're two people again. Don't you always think – hope that you'll be one person, and then find you're still two?"

"I feel very close to you."

"So do I to you," she said.

"Thank you."

"Thank *you*."

They laughed.

"Is this what you wanted?" she asked. "I mean last night."

"Not consciously."

"I wonder when it was settled," she brooded. "There's a moment when you needn't, and then there's another moment when you know nothing in the world could keep it from happening."

This had an experienced ring, and to his surprise he liked her even more. In his mood, which was passionately to repeat yet not recapitulate the past, it was right that it should be that way.

"I *am* rather a trollop," she said, following his thoughts. "I suppose that's why I didn't get on to Edna."

"Who is Edna?"

"The girl you thought was me. The one you phoned to – who lived across the road. She's moved to Santa Barbara."

"You mean she was a tart?"

"So it seems. She went to what you call call houses."

"That's funny."

"If she had been English, I'd have known right away. But she seemed like everyone else. She only told me just before she went away."

He saw her shiver and got up, putting the raincoat around her shoulders. He opened a closet and a pile of pillows and beach mattress fell out on the floor. There was a box of candles, and he lit them around the room, attaching the electric heater where the bulb had been.

"Why was Edna afraid of me?" he asked suddenly.

"Because you were a producer. She had some awful experience or a friend of hers did. Also, I think she was extremely stupid."

"How did you happen to know her?"

"She came over. Maybe she thought I was a fallen sister. She seemed quite pleasant. She said 'Call me Edna' all the time – 'Please call me Edna' – so finally I called her Edna and we were friends."

She got off the window seat so he could lay pillows along it and behind her.

"What can I do?" she said. "I'm a parasite."

"No, you're not." He put his arms around her. "Be still. Get warm."

They sat for a while quiet.

"I know why you liked me at first," she said. "Edna told me."

"What did she tell you?"

"That I looked like – Minna Davis. Several people have told me that."

He leant away from her and nodded.

"It's here," she said, putting her hands on her cheekbones and distorting her cheeks slightly. "Here and here."

"Yes," said Stahr. "It was very strange. You look more like she actually *looked* than how she was on the screen."

She got up, changing the subject with her gesture as if she were afraid of it.

"I'm warm now," she said. She went to the closet and peered in, came back wearing a little apron with a crystalline pattern like a snowfall. She stared around critically.

"Of course we've just moved in," she said, "and there's a sort of echo."

She opened the door of the veranda and pulled in two wicker chairs, drying them off. He watched her move, intently, yet half-afraid that her body would fail somewhere and break the spell. He had watched women in screen tests and seen their beauty vanish second by second, as if a lovely statue had begun to walk with the meagre joints of a paper doll. But Kathleen was ruggedly set on the balls of her feet – the fragility was, as it should be, an illusion.

"It's stopped raining," she said. "It rained the day I came. Such an awful rain – so loud – like horses weeing."

He laughed.

"You'll like it. Especially if you've got to stay here. Are you going to stay here? Can't you tell me now? What's the mystery?"

She shook her head.

"Not now – it's not worth telling."

"Come here then."

She came over and stood near him, and he pressed his cheek against the cool fabric of the apron.

"You're a tired man," she said, putting her hand in his hair.

"Not that way."

"I didn't mean that way," she said hastily. "I meant you'll work yourself sick."

"Don't be a mother," he said.

Be a trollop, he thought. He wanted the pattern of his life broken. If he was going to die soon, like the two doctors said, he wanted to stop being Stahr for a while and hunt for love like men who had no gifts to give, like young nameless men who looked along the streets in the dark.

"You've taken off my apron," she said gently.

"Yes."

"Would anyone be passing along the beach? Shall we put out the candles?"

"No, don't put out the candles."

Afterwards she lay half on a white cushion and smiled up at him.

"I feel like Venus on the half-shell," she said.

"What made you think of that?"

"Look at me – isn't it Botticelli?"

"I don't know," he said smiling. "It is if you say so."

She yawned.

"I've had such a good time. And I'm very fond of you."

"You know a lot, don't you?"

"What do you mean?"

"Oh, from little things you've said. Or perhaps the way you say them."

She deliberated.

"Not much," she said. "I never went to a university, if that's what you mean. But the man I told you about knew everything and he had a passion for educating me. He made out schedules and made me take courses at the Sorbonne and go to museums. I picked up a little."

"What was he?"

"He was a painter of sorts and a hellcat. And a lot besides. He wanted me to read Spengler* – everything was for that. All the history and philosophy and harmony was all so I could read Spengler, and then I left him before we got to Spengler. At the end I think that was the chief reason he didn't want me to go."

"Who was Spengler?"

"I tell you we didn't get to him," she laughed, "and now I'm forgetting everything very patiently, because it isn't likely I'll ever meet anyone like him again."

"Oh, but you shouldn't forget," said Stahr, shocked. He had an intense respect for learning, a racial memory of the old shuls. "You shouldn't forget."

"It was just in place of babies."

"You could teach your babies," he said.

"Could I?"

"Sure you could. You could give it to them while they were young. When I want to know anything, I've got to ask some drunken writer. Don't throw it away."

"All right," she said, getting up. "I'll tell it to my children. But it's so endless – the more you know, the more there is just beyond, and it keeps on coming. This man could have been anything if he hadn't been a coward and a fool."

"But you were in love with him."

"Oh, yes – with all my heart." She looked through the window, shading her eyes. "It's light out there. Let's go down to the beach."

He jumped up, exclaiming:

"Why, I think it's the grunion!"

"What?"

"It's tonight. It's in all the papers." He hurried out the door, and she heard him open the door of the car. Presently he returned with a newspaper.

"It's at ten sixteen. That's five minutes."

"An eclipse or something?"

"Very punctual fish," he said. "Leave your shoes and stockings and come with me."

It was a fine blue night. The tide was at the turn, and the little silver fish rocked offshore waiting for 10.16. A few seconds after the time they came swarming in with the tide, and Stahr and Kathleen stepped over them barefoot as they flicked slip-slop on the sand. A Negro man came along the shore towards them, collecting the grunion quickly, like twigs, into two pails. They came in twos and threes and platoons and companies, relentless and exalted and scornful, round the great bare feet of the intruders, as they had come before Sir Francis Drake had nailed his plaque to the boulder on the shore.*

"I wish for another pail," the Negro man said, resting a moment.

"You've come a long way out," said Stahr.

"I used to go to Malibu, but they don't like it, those moving-picture people."

A wave came in and forced them back, receded swiftly, leaving the sand alive again.

"Is it worth the trip?" Stahr asked.

"I don't figure it that way. I really come out to read some Emerson.* Have you ever read him?"

"I have," said Kathleen. "Some."

"I've got him inside my shirt. I got some Rosicrucian* literature with me too, but I'm fed up with them."

The wind had changed a little – the waves were stronger farther down, and they walked along the foaming edge of the water.

"What's your work?" the Negro asked Stahr.

"I work for the pictures."

"Oh." After a moment he added, "I never go to movies."

"Why not?" asked Stahr sharply.

"There's no profit. I never let my children go."

Stahr watched him, and Kathleen watched Stahr protectively.

"Some of them are good," she said, against a wave of spray, but he did not hear her. She felt she could contradict him and said it again, and this time he looked at her indifferently.

"Are the Rosicrucian brotherhood against pictures?" asked Stahr.

"Seems as if they don't know what they *are* for. One week they for one thing and next week for another."

Only the little fish were certain. Half an hour had gone, and still they came. The Negro's two pails were full, and finally he went off over the beach towards the road, unaware that he had rocked an industry.

Stahr and Kathleen walked back to the house, and she thought how to drive his momentary blues away.

"Poor old Sambo," she said.

"What?"

"Don't you call them poor old Sambo?"

"We don't call them anything especially." After a moment, he said, "They have pictures of their own."

In the house she drew on her shoes and stockings before the heater.

"I like California better," she said deliberately. "I think I was a bit sex-starved."

"That wasn't quite all, was it?"

"You know it wasn't."

"It's nice to be near you."

She gave a little sigh as she stood up, so small that he did not notice it.

"I don't want to lose you now," he said. "I don't know what you think of me or whether you think of me at all. As you've probably guessed, my heart's in the grave" – he hesitated, wondering if this was quite true – "but you're the most attractive woman I've met since I don't know when. I can't stop looking at you. I don't know now exactly the colour of your eyes, but they make me sorry for everyone in the world—"

"Stop it, stop it!" she cried laughing. "You'll have me looking in the mirror for weeks. My eyes aren't any colour – they're just eyes to see with, and I'm just as ordinary as I can be. I have nice teeth for an English girl—"

"You have beautiful teeth."

"—but I couldn't hold a candle to these girls I see here—"

"*You* stop it," he said. "What I said is true, and I'm a cautious man."

She stood motionless a moment – thinking. She looked at him, then she looked back into herself, then at him again – then she gave up her thought.

"We must go," she said.

* * *

Now they were different people as they started back. Four times they had driven along the shore road today, each time a different pair. Curiosity, sadness and desire were behind them now; this was a true returning – to themselves and all their past and future and the encroaching presence of tomorrow. He asked her to sit close in the car, and she did, but they did not seem close, because for that you have to seem to be growing closer. Nothing stands still. It was on his tongue to ask her to come to the house he rented and sleep there tonight – but he felt that it would make him sound lonely. As the car climbed the hill to her house, Kathleen looked for something behind the seat cushion.

"What have you lost?"

"It might have fallen out," she said, feeling through her purse in the darkness.

"What was it?"

"An envelope."

"Was it important?"

"No."

But when they got to her house and Stahr turned on the dashboard light, she helped take the cushions out and look again.

"It doesn't matter," she said, as they walked to the door. "What's your address where you really live?"

"Just Bel Air. There's no number."

"Where is Bel Air?"

"It's a sort of development, near Santa Monica. But you'd better call me at the studio."

"All right… goodnight, Mr Stahr."

"*Mister* Stahr," he repeated, astonished.

She corrected herself gently.

"Well, then, goodnight, Stahr. Is that better?"

He felt as though he had been pushed away a little.

"As you like," he said. He refused to let the aloofness communicate itself. He kept looking at her and moved his head from side to side in her own gesture, saying without words: "You know what's happened to me." She sighed. Then she came into his arms and for a moment was his again completely. Before anything could change, Stahr whispered goodnight and turned away and went to his car.

Winding down the hill, he listened inside himself as if something by an unknown composer, powerful and strange and strong, was about to be played for the first time. The theme would be stated presently, but because the composer was always new, he would not recognize it as the theme right away. It would come in some such guise as the auto horns from the Technicolor boulevards below, or be barely audible, a tattoo on the muffled drum of the moon. He strained to hear it, knowing only that music was beginning, new music that he liked and did not understand. It was hard to react to what one could entirely compass – this was new and confusing, nothing one could shut off in the middle and supply the rest from an old score.

Also, and persistently, and bound up with the other, there was the Negro on the sand. He was waiting at home for Stahr, with his pails of silver fish, and he would be waiting at the studio in the morning. He had said that he did not allow his children to listen to Stahr's story. He was prejudiced and wrong, and he must be shown somehow, some way. A picture, many pictures, a decade of pictures, must be made to show him he was wrong. Since he had spoken, Stahr had thrown four pictures out of his plans – one that was going into production this week. They were borderline pictures in point of interest, but at least he submitted the borderline pictures to the Negro and found them trash. And he put back on his list a difficult picture that he had tossed to the wolves, to Brady and Marcus and the rest, to get his way on something else. He rescued it for the Negro man.

When he drove up to his door, the porch lights went on, and his Filipino came down the steps to put away the car. In the library, Stahr found a list of phone calls:

La Borwitz
Marcus
Harlow
Reinmund
Fairbanks
Brady
Colman
Skouras
*Fleishacker, etc.**

The Filipino came into the room with a letter.

"This fell out of the car," he said.

"Thanks," said Stahr. "I was looking for it."

"Will you be running a picture tonight, Mr Stahr?"

"No, thanks – you can go to bed."

The letter, to his surprise, was addressed to Monroe Stahr, Esq. He started to open it – then it occurred to him that she had wanted to recapture it, and possibly to withdraw it. If she had had a phone, he would have called her for permission before opening it. He held it for a moment. It had been written before they met – it was odd to think that whatever it said was now invalidated; it possessed the interest of a souvenir by representing a mood that was gone.

Still he did not like to read it without asking her. He put it down beside a pile of scripts and sat down with the top script in his lap. He was proud of resisting his first impulse to open the letter. It seemed to prove that he was not "losing his head". He had never lost his head about Minna, even in the beginning – it had been the most appropriate and regal match imaginable. She had loved him always and, just before she died, all unwilling and surprised, his tenderness had burst and surged forward and he had been in love with her. In love with Minna and death together – with the world in which she looked so alone that he wanted to go with her there.

But "falling for dames" had never been an obsession – his brother had gone to pieces over a dame, or rather over dame after dame after dame. But Stahr, in his younger days, had them once and never more than once – like one drink. He had quite another sort of adventure reserved for his mind – something better than a series of emotional sprees. Like many brilliant men, he had grown up dead cold. Beginning at about twelve, probably, with the total rejection common to those of extraordinary mental powers, the "See here: this is all wrong – a mess – all a lie – and a sham…", he swept it all away, everything, as men of his type do, and then instead of being a son-of-a-bitch as most of them are, he looked around at the barrenness that was left and said to himself, "*This* will never do." And so he had learnt tolerance, kindness, forbearance and even affection, like lessons.

The Filipino boy brought in a carafe of water and bowls of nuts and fruit, and said goodnight. Stahr opened the first script and began to read.

He read for three hours – stopping from time to time, editing without a pencil. Sometimes he looked up, warm from some very vague happy thought that was not in the script, and it took him a minute each time to remember what it was. Then he knew it was Kathleen, and he looked at the letter – it was nice to have a letter.

It was three o'clock when a vein began to bump in the back of his hand, signalling that it was time to quit. Kathleen was really far away now with the waning night – the different aspects of her telescoped into the memory of a single thrilling stranger, bound to him only by a few slender hours. It seemed perfectly all right to open the letter.

Dear Mr Stahr,
In half an hour I will be keeping my date with you. When we say goodbye I will hand you this letter. It is to tell you that I am to be married soon and that I won't be able to see you after today.

I should have told you last night but it didn't seem to concern you. And it would seem silly to spend this beautiful afternoon telling you about it and watching your interest fade. Let it fade all at once – now. I will have told you enough to convince you that I am Nobody's Prize Potato. (I have just learnt that expression – from my hostess of last night, who called and stayed an hour. She seems to believe that everyone is Nobody's Prize Potato – except you. I think I am supposed to tell you she thinks this, so give her a job if you can.)

I am very flattered that anyone who sees so many lovely women... I can't finish this sentence but you know what I mean. And I will be late if I don't go to meet you right now.
With all good wishes,
Kathleen Moore

Stahr's first feeling was like fear; his second thought was that the letter was invalidated – she had even tried to retrieve it. But then he remembered "Mister Stahr" just at the end, and that she had asked him his address – she had probably already written another letter which would also say goodbye. Illogically he was shocked by the letter's indifference to what had happened later. He read it again, realizing that it foresaw nothing. Yet in front of the house she had decided to let it stand, belittling everything that had happened, curving her mind away from the fact that there had been no other man in her consciousness that afternoon. But he could not even believe this now, and the whole adventure began to peel away even as he recapitulated it searchingly to himself. The car, the hill, the hat, the music, the letter itself, blew off like the scraps of tar paper from the rubble of his house. And Kathleen departed, packing up her remembered gestures, her softly moving head, her sturdy eager body, her bare feet in the wet swirling sand. The skies paled and faded – the wind and rain turned dreary, washing the silver fish back to sea. It was only one more day, and nothing was left except the pile of scripts upon the table.

He went upstairs. Minna died again on the first landing, and he forgot her lingeringly and miserably again, step by step to the top. The empty floor stretched around him – the doors with no one sleeping behind. In his room, Stahr took off his tie, untied his shoes and sat on the side of his bed. It was all closed out, except for something that he could not remember; then he remembered: her car was still down in the parking lot of the hotel. He set his clock to give him six hours' sleep.

* * *

This is Cecilia taking up the story. I think it would be most interesting to follow my own movements at this point, as this is a time in my life that I am ashamed of. What people are ashamed of usually makes a good story.

When I sent Wylie over to Martha Dodd's table, he had no success in finding out who the girl was, but it had suddenly become my chief interest in life. Also, I guessed – correctly – that it would be Martha Dodd's. To have had at your table a girl who is admired by royalty, who may be tagged for a coronet in our little feudal system – and not even know her name!

I had only a speaking acquaintance with Martha, and it would be too obvious to approach her directly, but I went out to the studio Monday and dropped in on Jane Meloney.

Jane Meloney was quite a friend of mine. I thought of her rather as a child thinks of a family dependant. I knew she was a writer, but I grew up thinking that writer and secretary

were the same, except that a writer usually smelt of cocktails
and came more often to meals. They were spoken of the same
way when they were not around – except for a species called
playwrights, who came from the East. These were treated with
respect if they did not stay long – if they did, they sank with
the others into the white-collar class.

Jane's office was in the "old writers' building". There was
one on every lot, a row of iron maidens left over from silent
days and still resounding with the dull moans of cloistered
hacks and bums. There was the story of the new producer who
had gone down the line one day and then reported excitedly
to the head office.

"Who are those men?"

"They're supposed to be writers."

"I thought so. Well, I watched them for ten minutes and there
were two of them that didn't write a line."

Jane was at her typewriter, about to break off for lunch. I
told her frankly that I had a rival.

"It's a dark horse," I said. "I can't even find out her name."

"Oh," said Jane. "Well, maybe I know something about that.
I heard something from somebody."

The somebody, of course, was her nephew, Ned Sollinger,
Stahr's office boy. He had been her pride and hope. She had
sent him through New York University, where he played on the
football team. Then in his first year at medical school, after
a girl turned him down, he dissected out the least publicized
section of a lady corpse and sent it to the girl. Don't ask me
why. In disgrace with fortune and men's eyes,* he had begun
life at the bottom again, and was still there.

"What do you know?" I asked.

"It was the night of the earthquake. She fell into the lake on the back lot, and he dove in and saved her life. Someone else told me it was his balcony she jumped off of and broke her arm."

"Who was she?"

"Well, that's funny too—"

Her phone rang, and I waited restlessly during a long conversation she had with Joe Reinmund. He seemed to be trying to find out over the phone how good she was or whether she had ever written any pictures at all. And she was reputed to have been on the set the day Griffith invented the close-up! While he talked she groaned silently, writhed, made faces into the receiver, held it all in her lap so that the voice reached her faintly – and kept up a side chatter to me.

"What is *he* doing – killing time between appointments?... He's asked me every one of these questions ten times... that's all on a memorandum I sent him..."

And into the phone:

"If this goes up to Monroe, it won't be my doing. I want to go right through to the end."

She shut her eyes in agony again.

"Now he's casting it... he's casting the minor characters... he's going to have Buddy Ebsen... My God, he just hasn't anything to do... now he's on Harry Davenport – he means Donald Crisp...* he's got a big casting directory open in his lap and I can hear him turn the pages... he's a big important man this morning, a second Stahr, and for Christ's sake I've got two scenes to do before lunch."

Reinmund quit finally or was interrupted at his end. A waiter came in from the commissary with Jane's luncheon and a Coca-Cola for me – I wasn't lunching that summer. Jane wrote down one sentence on her typewriter before she ate. It interested me the way she wrote. One day I was there when she and a young man had just lifted a story out of *The Saturday Evening Post* – changing the characters and all. Then they began to write it, making each line answer the line before it, and of course it sounded just like people do in life when they're straining to be anything – funny or gentle or brave. I always wanted to see that one on the screen, but I missed it somehow.

I found her as lovable as a cheap old toy. She made three thousand a week, and her husbands all drank and beat her nearly to death. But today I had an axe to grind.

"You don't know her name?" I persisted.

"Oh..." said Jane, "that. Well, he kept calling her up afterwards, and he told Katy Doolan it was the wrong name after all."

"I think he found her," I said. "Do you know Martha Dodd?"

"Hasn't that little girl had a tough break, though!" she exclaimed with ready theatrical sympathy.

"Could you possibly invite her to lunch tomorrow?"

"Oh, I think she gets enough to eat all right. There's a Mexican—"

I explained that my motives were not charitable. Jane agreed to cooperate. She called Martha Dodd.

We had lunch next day at the Bev Brown Derby, a languid restaurant, patronized for its food by clients who always look as if they'd like to lie down. There is some animation at lunch, where the women put on a show for the first five minutes after they eat, but we were a tepid threesome. I should have come right out with my curiosity. Martha Dodd was an agricultural girl, who had never quite understood what had happened to her and had nothing to show for it except a washed-out look about the eyes. She still believed that the life she had tasted was reality and this was only a long waiting.

"I had a beautiful place in 1928," she told us. "Thirty acres, with a miniature golf course and a pool and a gorgeous view. All spring I was up to my ass in daisies."

I ended by asking her to come over and meet Father. This was pure penance for having had "a mixed motive" and being ashamed of it. One doesn't mix motives in Hollywood – it is confusing. Everybody understands, and the climate wears you down. A mixed motive is conspicuous waste.

Jane left us at the studio gate, disgusted by my cowardice. Martha had worked up inside to a pitch about her career – not a very high pitch, because of seven years of neglect, but a sort of nervous acquiescence, and I was going to speak strongly to Father. They never did anything for people like Martha, who had made them so much money at one time. They let them slip away into misery eked out with extra work – it would have been kinder to ship them out of town. And Father was being so proud of me this summer. I had to keep him from telling everybody just how I had been brought up so as to produce such a perfect jewel. And Bennington – oh, what an exclusive – dear God, my heart. I assured him there was the usual proportion of natural-born skivvies and biddies tastefully concealed by throw-overs from Sex Fifth Avenue,* but Father had worked himself up to practically an alumnus. "You've had everything," he used to say happily. Everything included roughly the two years in Florence, where I managed against heavy odds to be the only virgin in school, and the courtesy debut in Boston, Massachusetts. I was a veritable flower of the fine old cost-and-gross aristocracy.

So I knew he would do something for Martha Dodd and, as he went into his office, I had great dreams of doing something for Johnny Swanson, the cowboy, too, and Evelyn Brent, and all sorts of discarded flowers. Father was a charming and sympathetic man – except for that time I had seen him unexpectedly in New York – and there was something touching about his being my father. After all, he was *my* father – he would do anything in the world for me.

Only Rosemary Schmiel was in the outer office, and she was on Birdy Peter's phone. She waved for me to sit down, but I was full of my plans and, telling Martha to take it easy, I pressed the clicker under Rosemary's desk and went towards the opened door.

"Your father's in conference," Rosemary called. "Not in conference, but I ought to…"

By this time I was through the door and a little vestibule and another door, and caught Father in his shirtsleeves, very sweaty and trying to open a window. It was a hot day, but I hadn't realized it was that hot, and thought he was ill.

"No, I'm all right," he said. "What is it?"

I told him. I told him the whole theory of people like Martha Dodd, walking up and down his office. How could he use them and guarantee them regular employment? He seemed to take me up excitedly and kept nodding and agreeing, and I felt closer to him than I had for a long time. I came close and kissed him on his cheek. He was trembling and his shirt was soaked through.

"You're not well," I said, "or you're in some sort of stew."

"No, I'm not at all."

"What is it?"

"Oh, it's Monroe," he said. "That goddam little Vine Street Jesus! He's in my hair night and day!"

"What's happened?" I asked, very much cooler.

"Oh, he sits like a little goddamn priest or rabbi and says what he'll do and he won't do. I can't tell you now – I'm half crazy. Why don't you go along?"

"I won't have you like this."

"Go along, I tell you!" I sniffed, but he never drank.

"Go and brush your hair," I said. "I want you to see Martha Dodd."

"In here! I'd never get rid of her."

"Out there then. Go wash up first. Put on another shirt."

With an exaggerated gesture of despair, he went into the little bathroom adjoining. It was hot in the office as if it had been closed for hours, and maybe that was making him sick, so I opened two more windows.

"You go along," Father called from behind the closed door of the bathroom. "I'll be there presently."

"Be awfully nice to her," I said. "No charity."

As if it were Martha speaking for herself, a long low moan came from somewhere in the room. I was startled – then transfixed, as it came again, not from the bathroom where Father was, not from outside, but from a closet in the wall across from me. How I was brave enough I don't know, but I ran across to it and opened it, and Father's secretary, Birdy Peters, tumbled out stark naked – just like a corpse in the movies. With her came a gust of stifling, stuffy air. She flopped sideways on the floor, with the one hand still clutching some clothes, and lay on the floor bathed in sweat – just as Father came in from the bathroom. I could feel him standing behind me, and without turning I knew exactly how he looked, for I had surprised him before.

"Cover her up," I said, covering her up myself with a rug from the couch. "Cover her *up*!"

I left the office. Rosemary Schmiel saw my face as I came out and responded with a terrified expression. I never saw her again or Birdy Peters either. As Martha and I went out, Martha asked: "What's the matter, dear?" – and when I didn't say anything: "You did your best. Probably it was the wrong time. I'll tell you what I'll do. I'll take you to see a very nice English girl. Did you see the girl that Stahr danced with at our table the other night?"

So at the price of a little immersion in the family drains I had what I wanted.

* * *

I don't remember much about our call. She wasn't at home was one reason. The screen door of her house was unlocked, and Martha went in, calling "Kathleen" with bright familiarity. The room we saw was bare and formal as a hotel; there were flowers about, but they did not look like sent flowers. Also, Martha found a note on the table, which said: "Leave the dress. Have gone looking for a job. Will drop by tomorrow."

Martha read it twice, but it didn't seem to be for Stahr, and we waited five minutes. People's houses are very still when they are gone. Not that I expect them to be jumping around, but I leave the observation for what it's worth. Very still. Prim almost, with just a fly holding down the place and paying no attention to you, and the corner of a curtain blowing.

"I wonder what kind of a job," said Martha. "Last Sunday she went somewhere with Stahr."

But I was no longer interested. It seemed awful to be here – producer's blood, I thought in horror. And in quick panic I pulled her out into the placid sunshine. It was no use – I felt just black and awful. I had always been proud of my body – I had a way of thinking of it as geometric, which made everything it did seem all right. And there was probably not any kind of place, including churches and office and shrines, where people had not embraced – but no one had ever stuffed me naked into a hole in the wall in the middle of a business day.

* * *

"If you were in a drugstore," said Stahr, "having a prescription filled—"

"You mean a chemist's?" Boxley asked.

"If you were in a chemist's," conceded Stahr, "and you were getting a prescription for some member of your family who was very sick—"

"Very ill?" queried Boxley.

"Very ill. *Then*, whatever caught your attention through the window, whatever distracted you and held you would probably be material for pictures."

"A murder outside the window, you mean."

"There you go," said Stahr, smiling. "It might be a spider working on the pane."

"Of course – I see."

"I'm afraid you don't, Mr Boxley. You see it for *your* medium, but not for ours. You keep the spiders for yourself and you try to pin the murders on us."

"I might as well leave," said Boxley. "I'm no good to you. I've been here three weeks and I've accomplished nothing. I make suggestions, but no one writes them down."

"I want you to stay. Something in you doesn't like pictures, doesn't like telling a story this way—"

"It's such a damned bother," exploded Boxley. "You can't let yourself go..."

He checked himself. He knew that Stahr, the helmsman, was finding time for him in the middle of a constant stiff blow – that they were talking in the always creaking rigging of a ship sailing in great awkward tacks along an open sea. Or else – it seemed at times – they were in a huge quarry – where even the newly cut marble bore the tracery of old pediments, half-obliterated inscriptions of the past.

"I keep wishing you could start over," Boxley said. "It's this mass production."

"That's the condition," said Stahr. "There's always some lousy condition. We're making a life of Rubens – suppose I asked you to do portraits of rich dopes like Bill Brady and me and Gary Cooper* and Marcus when you wanted to paint Jesus Christ? Wouldn't you feel you had a condition? Our condition is that we have to take people's own favourite folklore and dress it up and give it back to them. Anything beyond that is sugar. So won't you give us some sugar, Mr Boxley?"

Boxley knew he could sit with Wylie White tonight at the Troc raging at Stahr, but he had been reading Lord Charnwood* and he recognized that Stahr, like Lincoln, was a leader carrying on a long war on many fronts; almost single-handed he had moved pictures sharply forward through a decade, to a point where the content of the "A productions" was wider and richer than that of the stage. Stahr was an artist only, as Mr Lincoln was a general, perforce and as a layman.

"Come down to La Borwitz's office with me," said Stahr. "They sure need some sugar there."

In La Borwitz's office, two writers, a shorthand secretary and a hushed supervisor, sat in a tense smoky stalemate, where Stahr had left them three hours before. He looked at the faces one after another and found nothing. La Borwitz spoke with awed reverence for his defeat.

"We've just got too many characters, Monroe."

Stahr snorted affably.

"That's the principal idea of the picture."

He took some change out of his pocket, looked up at the suspended light and tossed up half a dollar, which clanked into the bowl. He looked at the coins in his hands and selected a quarter.

La Borwitz watched miserably; he knew this was a favourite trick of Stahr's and he saw the sands running out. At the moment everyone's back was towards him. Suddenly he brought up his hands from their placid position under the desk and threw them high in the air, so high that they seemed to leave his wrist – and then he caught them neatly as they were descending. After that he felt better. He was in control.

One of the writers had taken out some coins, also, and presently rules were defined. "You have to toss your coin through the chains without hitting them. Whatever falls into the light is the kitty."

They played for half an hour – all except Boxley, who sat aside and dug into the script, and the secretary, who kept tally. She calculated the cost of the four men's time, arriving at a figure of sixteen hundred dollars. At the end, La Borwitz was winner by $5.50, and a janitor brought in a stepladder to take the money out of the light.

Boxley spoke up suddenly.

"You have the stuffings of a turkey here," he said.

"What!"

"It's not pictures."

They looked at him in astonishment. Stahr concealed a smile.

"So we've got a real picture man here!" exclaimed La Borwitz.

"A lot of beautiful speeches," said Boxley boldly, "but no situations. After all, you know, it's not going to be a novel. And it's too long. I can't exactly describe how I feel, but it's not quite right. And it leaves me cold."

He was giving them back what had been handed him for three weeks. Stahr turned away, watching the others out of the corner of his eye.

"We don't need *less* characters," said Boxley. "We need *more*. As I see it, that's the idea."

"That's the idea," said the writers.

"Yes – that's the idea," said La Borwitz.

Boxley was inspired by the attention he had created.

"Let each character see himself in the other's place," he said. "The policeman is about to arrest the thief when he sees that the thief actually has *his* face. I mean, show it that way. You could almost call the thing *Put Yourself in My Place*."

Suddenly they were at work again – taking up this new theme in turn like hepcats in a swing band and going to town with it. They might throw it out again tomorrow, but life had come back for a moment. Pitching the coins had done it as much as Boxley. Stahr had recreated the proper atmosphere – never consenting to be a driver of the driven, but feeling like and acting like and even sometimes looking like a small boy getting up a show.

He left them, touching Boxley on the shoulder in passing – a deliberate accolade – he didn't want them to gang up on him and break his spirit in an hour.

* * *

Doctor Baer was waiting in his inner office. With him was a coloured man with a portable cardiograph like a huge suitcase. Stahr called it the lie detector. Stahr stripped to the waist, and the weekly examination began.

"How've you been feeling?"

"Oh – the usual," said Stahr.

"Been hard at it? Getting any sleep?"

"No – about five hours. If I go to bed early, I just lie there."

"Take the sleeping pills."

"The yellow one gives me a hangover."

"Take two red ones, then."

"That's a nightmare."

"Take one of each – the yellow first."

"All right – I'll try. How've *you* been?"

"Say – I take care of myself, Monroe, I save myself."

"The hell you do – you're up all night sometimes."

"Then I sleep all next day."

After ten minutes, Baer said:

"Seems OK. The blood pressure's up five points."

"Good," said Stahr. "That's good, isn't it?"

"That's good. I'll develop the cardiographs tonight. When are you coming away with me?"

"Oh, sometime," said Stahr lightly. "In about six weeks things'll ease up."

Baer looked at him with a genuine liking that had grown over three years.

"You got better in Thirty-three when you laid up," he said. "Even for three weeks."

"I will again."

No he wouldn't, Baer thought. With Minna's help he had enforced a few short rests years ago, and lately he had hinted around, trying to find who Stahr considered his closest friends. Who could take him away and keep him away? It would almost surely be useless. He was due to die very soon now. Within six months one could say definitely. What was the use of developing the cardiograms? You couldn't persuade a man like Stahr to stop and lie down and look at the sky for six months. He would much rather die. He said differently, but what it added up to was the definite urge towards total exhaustion that he had run into before. Fatigue was a drug as well as a poison, and Stahr apparently derived some rare almost physical pleasure from working light-headed with weariness. It was a perversion of the life force he had seen before, but he had almost stopped trying to interfere with it. He had cured a man or so – a hollow triumph of killing and preserving the shell.

"You hold your own," he said.

They exchanged a glance. Did Stahr know? Probably. But he did not know when – he did not know how soon now.

"If I hold my own, I can't ask more," said Stahr.

The coloured man had finished packing the apparatus.

"Next week same time?"

"OK, Bill," said Stahr. "Goodbye."

As the door closed, Stahr switched open the dictagraph. Miss Doolan's voice came through immediately.

"Do you know a Miss Kathleen Moore?"

"What do you mean?" he asked, startled.

"A Miss Kathleen Moore is on the line. She said you asked her to call."

"Well, my God!" he exclaimed. He was swept with indignant rapture. It had been five days – this would never do at all.

"She's on now?"

"Yes."

"Well, all right then."

In a moment he heard the voice up close to him.

"Are you married?" he asked, low and surly.

"No, not yet."

His memory blocked out her face and form – as he sat down, she seemed to lean down to his desk, keeping level with his eyes.

"What's on your mind?" he asked in the same surly voice. It was hard to talk that way.

"You did find the letter?" she asked.

"Yes. It turned up that night."

"That's what I want to speak to you about."

He found an attitude at length – he was outraged.

"What is there to talk about?" he demanded.

"I tried to write you another letter, but it wouldn't write."

"I know that too."

There was a pause.

"Oh, cheer up!" she said surprisingly. "This doesn't sound like you. It *is* Stahr, isn't it? That very nice Mr Stahr?"

"I feel a little outraged," he said, almost pompously. "I don't see the use of this. I had at least a pleasant memory of you."

"I don't believe it's you," she said. "Next thing you'll wish me luck." Suddenly she laughed: "Is this what you planned to say? I know how awful it gets when you plan to say anything—"

"I never expected to hear from you again," he said with dignity; but it was no use, she laughed again – a woman's laugh that is like a child's, just one syllable, a crow and a cry of delight.

"Do you know how you make me feel?" she demanded. "Like a day in London during a caterpillar plague when a hot furry thing dropped in my mouth."

"I'm sorry."

"Oh, please wake up," she begged. "I want to see you. I can't explain things on the phone. It was no fun for me either, you understand."

"I'm very busy. There's a sneak preview in Glendale tonight."

"Is that an invitation?"

"George Boxley, the English writer, is going with me." He surprised himself. "Do you want to come along?"

"How could we talk?"

She considered. "Why don't you call for me afterwards," she suggested. "We could ride around."

Miss Doolan on the huge dictagraph was trying to cut in on the line with a shooting director – the only interruption ever permitted. He flipped the button and called "Wait" impatiently into the machine.

"About eleven?" Kathleen was saying confidentially.

The idea of "riding around" seemed so unwise that if he could have thought of the words to refuse her he would have spoken them, but he did not want to be the caterpillar. Suddenly he had no attitude left except the sense that the day, at least, was complete. He had an evening – a beginning, a middle and an end.

* * *

He rapped on the screen door, heard her call from inside and stood waiting where the level fell away. From below came the whir of a lawnmower – a man was cutting his grass at midnight. The moon was so bright that Stahr could see him plainly, a hundred feet off and down, as he stopped and rested on the handle before pushing it back across his garden. There was a midsummer restlessness abroad – early August with imprudent loves and impulsive crimes. With little more to expect from summer, one tried anxiously to live in the present – or, if there was no present, to invent one.

She came at last. She was all different and delighted. She wore a suit with a skirt that she kept hitching up as they walked down to the car with a brave, gay, stimulating, reckless air of "Tighten up your belt, baby. Let's get going." Stahr had brought his limousine with the chauffeur, and the intimacy of the four walls whisking them along a new curve in the dark took away any strangeness at once. In its way, the little trip they made was one of the best times he had ever had in his life. It was certainly one of the times when, if he knew he was going to die, it was not tonight.

She told him her story. She sat beside him cool and gleaming for a while, spinning on excitedly, carrying him to far places with her, meeting and knowing the people she had known. The story was vague at first. "This Man" was the one she had loved and lived with. "This American" was the one who had rescued her when she was sinking into a quicksand.

"Who is he – the American?"

Oh, names – what did they matter? No one important like Stahr, not rich. He had lived in London and now they would live out here. She was going to be a good wife, a real person. He was getting a divorce – not just on account of her – but that was the delay.

"But the first man?" asked Stahr. "How did you get into that?"

Oh, that was a blessing at first. From sixteen to twenty-one the thing was to eat. The day her stepmother presented her at Court they had one shilling to eat with so as not to feel faint. Sixpence apiece, but the stepmother watched while she ate. After a few months the stepmother died, and she would have sold out for that shilling, but she was too weak to go into the streets. London can be harsh – oh, quite.

Was there nobody?

There were friends in Ireland who sent butter. There was a soup kitchen. There was a visit to an uncle, who made advances to her when she had a full stomach, and she held out and got fifty pounds out of him for not telling his wife.

"Couldn't you work?" Stahr asked.

"I worked. I sold cars. Once I sold a car."

"But couldn't you get a regular job?"

"It's hard – it's different. There was a feeling that people like me forced other people out of jobs. A woman struck me when I tried to get a job as chambermaid in a hotel."

"But you were presented at Court?"

"That was my stepmother who did that – on an off-chance. I was nobody. My father was shot by the Black-and-Tans* in Twenty-two when I was a child. He wrote a book called *Last Blessing*. Did you ever read it?"

"I don't read."

"I wish you'd buy it for the movies. It's a good little book. I still get a royalty from it – ten shillings a year."

Then she met "The Man" and they travelled the world around. She had been to all the places that Stahr made movies of, and lived in cities whose name he had never heard. Then The Man went to seed, drinking and sleeping with the house-maids and trying to force her off on his friends. They all tried to make her stick with him. They said she had saved him and should cleave to him longer now, indefinitely, to the end. It was her duty. They brought enormous pressure to bear. But she had met The American, and so finally she ran away.

"You should have run away before."

"Well, you see, it was difficult." She hesitated, and plunged. "You see, I ran away from a king."

His moralities somehow collapsed – she had managed to top him. A confusion of thoughts raced through his head – one of them a faint old credo that all royalty was diseased.

"It wasn't the King of England," she said. "My king was out of a job as he used to say. There are lots of kings in London." She laughed – then added, almost defiantly, "He was very attractive until he began drinking and raising hell."

"What was he king of?"

She told him – and Stahr visualized the face out of old newsreels.

"He was a very learned man," she said. "He could have taught all sorts of subjects. But he wasn't much like a king. Not nearly as much as you. None of them were."

This time Stahr laughed.

"You know what I mean. They all felt old-fashioned. Most of them tried so hard to keep up with things. They were always advised to keep up with things. One was a syndicalist, for instance. And one used to carry around a couple of clippings about a tennis tournament when he was in the semi-finals. I saw those clippings a dozen times."

They rode through Griffith Park and out past the dark studios of Burbank, past the airports and along the way to Pasadena past the neon signs of roadside cabarets. Up in his head he wanted her, but it was late and just the ride was an overwhelming joy. They held hands and once she came close into his arms saying, "Oh, you're *so* nice. I *do* like to be with you." But her mind was divided – this was not his night as the Sunday afternoon had been his. She was absorbed in herself, stung into excitement by telling of her own adventures; he could not help wondering if he was getting the story she had saved up for The American.

"How long have you known The American?" he asked.

"Oh, I knew him for several months. We used to meet. We understood each other. He used to say, 'It looks like a cinch from now on.'"

"Then why did you call me up?"

She hesitated.

"I wanted to see you once more. Then, *too* – he was supposed to arrive today, but last night he wired that he'd be another week. I wanted to talk to a friend – after all, you *are* my friend."

He wanted her very much now, but one part of his mind was cold and kept saying: she wants to see if I'm in love with her, if I want to marry her. Then she'd consider whether or not to throw this man over. She won't consider it till I've committed myself.

"Are you in love with The American?" he asked.

"Oh, yes. It's absolutely arranged. He saved my life and my reason. He's moving halfway round the world for me. I insisted on that."

"But are you in love with him?"

"Oh, yes. I'm in love with him."

The "Oh, yes" told him she was not – told him to speak for himself – that she would see. He took her in his arms and kissed her deliberately on the mouth and held her for a long time. It was so warm.

"Not tonight," she whispered.

"All right."

They passed over suicide bridge with the high new wire.

"I know what it is," she said, "but how stupid. English people don't kill themselves when they don't get what they want."

They turned around in the driveway of a hotel and started back. It was a dark night with no moon. The wave of desire had passed and neither spoke for a while. Her talk of kings had carried him oddly back in flashes to the pearly White Way of Main Street in Erie, Pennsylvania, when he was fifteen. There was a restaurant with lobsters in the window and green weeds and bright lights on a shell cavern, and beyond, behind a red curtain, the terribly strange brooding mystery of people and violin music. That was just before he left for New York. This girl reminded him of the fresh iced fishes and lobsters in the window. She was Beautiful Doll.* Minna had never been Beautiful Doll.

They looked at each other and her eyes asked, "Shall I marry The American?" He did not answer. After a while he said:

"Let's go somewhere for the weekend."

She considered.

"Are you talking about tomorrow?"

"I'm afraid I am."

"Well, I'll tell you tomorrow," she said.

"Tell me tonight. I'd be afraid—"

"—find a note in the car?" she laughed. "No, there's no note in the car. You know almost everything now."

"Almost everything."

"Yes – almost. A few little things."

He would have to know what they were. She would tell him tomorrow. He doubted – he wanted to doubt – if there had been a maze of philandering: a fixation had held her to The Man, the king, firmly and long. Three years of a highly anomalous position – one foot in the palace and one in the background. "You had to laugh a lot," she said. "I learnt to laugh a lot."

"He could have married you – like Mrs Simpson," Stahr said in protest.

"Oh, he was married. And he wasn't a romantic." She stopped herself.

"Am I?"

"Yes," she said, unwillingly, as if she were laying down a trump. "Part of you is. You're three or four different men, but each of them out in the open. Like all Americans."

"Don't start trusting Americans too implicitly," he said smiling. "They may be out in the open, but they change very fast."

She looked concerned.

"Do they?"

"Very fast and all at once," he said, "and nothing ever changes them back."

"You frighten me. I always had a great sense of security with Americans."

She seemed suddenly so alone that he took her hand.

"Where will we go tomorrow?" he said. "Maybe up in the mountains. I've got everything to do tomorrow, but I won't do any of it. We can start at four and get there by afternoon."

"I'm not sure. I seem to be a little mixed up. This doesn't seem to be quite the girl who came out to California for a new life."

He could have said it then, said, "It *is* a new life," for he knew it was, he knew he could not let her go now – but something else said to sleep on it as an adult, no romantic. And not to tell her till tomorrow. Still she was looking at him, her eyes wandering from his forehead to his chin and back again, and then up and down once more, with that odd, slowly waving motion of her head.

…It is your chance, Stahr. Better take it now. This is your girl. She can save you, she can worry you back to life. She will take looking after and you will grow strong to do it. But take her now – tell her and take her away. Neither of you knows it, but far away over the night The American has changed his plans. At this moment his train is speeding through Albuquerque; the schedule is accurate. The engineer is on time. In the morning he will be here.

…The chauffeur turned up the hill to Kathleen's house. It seemed warm even in darkness – wherever he had been near here was by way of being an enchanted place for Stahr: this limousine, the rising house at the beach, the very distances they had already covered together over the sprawled city. The hill they climbed now gave forth a sort of glow, a sustained sound that struck his soul alert with delight.

As he said goodbye he felt again that it was impossible to leave her, even for a few hours. There were only ten years between them, but he felt that madness about it akin to the love of an ageing man for a young girl. It was a deep and desperate time need, a clock ticking with his heart, and it urged him, against the whole logic of his life, to walk past her into the house now and say, "This is for ever."

Kathleen waited, irresolute herself – pink and silver frost waiting to melt with spring. She was a European, humble in the face of power, but there was a fierce self-respect that would only let her go so far. She had no illusions about the considerations that swayed princes.

"We'll go to the mountains tomorrow," said Stahr. Many thousands of people depended on his balanced judgement – you can suddenly blunt a quality you have lived by for twenty years.

He was very busy the next morning, Saturday. At two o'clock when he came from luncheon, there was a stack of telegrams – a company ship was lost in the Arctic; a star was in disgrace; a writer was suing for one million dollars. Jews were dead miserably beyond the sea. The last telegram stared up at him:

I was married at noon today. Goodbye; and on a sticker attached, *Send your answer by Western Union Telegram.*

Chapter 6

I KNEW NOTHING about any of this. I went up to Lake Louise, and when I came back didn't go near the studio. I think I would have started East in mid-August – if Stahr hadn't called me up one day at home.

"I want you to arrange something, Celia – I want to meet a Communist Party member."

"Which one?" I asked, somewhat startled.

"Any one."

"Haven't you got plenty out there?"

"I mean one of their organizers – from New York."

The summer before I had been all politics – I could probably have arranged a meeting with Harry Bridges.* But my boy had been killed in an auto accident after I went back to college, and I was out of touch with such things. I had heard there was a man from *The New Masses** around somewhere.

"Will you promise him immunity?" I asked, joking.

"Oh, yes," Stahr answered seriously. "I won't hurt him. Get one that can talk – tell him to bring one of his books along."

He spoke as if he wanted to meet a member of the "I AM" cult.*

"Do you want a blonde or a brunette?"

"Oh, get a man," he said hastily.

Hearing Stahr's voice cheered me up – since I had barged in on Father it had all seemed a paddling-about in thin spittle.

Stahr changed everything about it – changed the angle from which I saw it, changed the very air.

"I don't think your father ought to know," he said. "Can we pretend the man is a Bulgarian musician or something?"

"Oh, they don't dress up any more," I said.

It was harder to arrange than I thought – Stahr's negotiations with the Writers' Guild, which had continued over a year, were approaching a dead end. Perhaps they were afraid of being corrupted, and I was asked what Stahr's "proposition" was. Afterwards Stahr told me that he prepared for the meeting by running off the Russian revolutionary films that he had in his film library at home. He also ran off *Doctor Caligari* and Salvador Dalí's *Le Chien andalou*,* possibly suspecting that they had a bearing on the matter. He had been startled by the Russian films back in the Twenties, and on Wylie White's suggestion he had had the script department get him up a two-page "treatment" of the *Communist Manifesto*.*

But his mind was closed on the subject. He was a rationalist who did his own reasoning without benefit of books – and he had just managed to climb out of a thousand years of Jewry into the late eighteenth century. He could not bear to see it melt away – he cherished the parvenu's passionate loyalty to an imaginary past.

The meeting took place in what I called the "processed-leather room" – it was one of six done for us by a decorator from Sloane's years ago, and the term stuck in my head. It was *the* most decorator's room: an angora wool carpet the colour of dawn, the most delicate grey imaginable – you hardly dared walk on it – and the silver panelling and leather tables and creamy pictures and slim fragilities looked so easy to stain that we could not breathe hard in there, though it was wonderful to look into from the door when the windows were open and the curtains whimpered querulously against the breeze. It was a lineal descendant of the old American parlour that used to be closed except on Sundays. But it was exactly the room for the occasion, and I hoped that whatever happened would give it character and make it henceforth part of our house.

Stahr arrived first. He was white and nervous and troubled – except for his voice, which was always quiet and full of consideration. There was a brave personal quality in the way he would meet you – he would walk right up to you and put aside something that was in the way, and grow to know you all over as if he couldn't help himself. I kissed him for some reason, and took him into the processed-leather room.

"When do you go back to college?" he asked.

We had been over this fascinating ground before.

"Would you like me if I were a little shorter?" I asked. "I could wear low heels and plaster down my hair."

"Let's have dinner tonight," he suggested. "People will think I'm your father but I don't mind."

"I *love* old men," I assured him. "Unless the man has a crutch, I feel it's just a boy-and-girl affair."

"Have you had many of those?"

"Enough."

"People fall in and out of love all the time, don't they?"

"Every three years or so, Fanny Brice* says. I just read it in the paper."

"I wonder how they manage it," he said. "I know it's true because I see them. But they look so *convinced* every time.

And then suddenly they don't look convinced. But they get convinced all over."

"You've been making too many movies."

"I wonder if they're as convinced the second time or the third time or the fourth time," he persisted.

"More each time," I said. "Most of all the last time."

He thought this over and seemed to agree.

"I suppose so. Most of all the last time."

I didn't like the way he said this, and I suddenly saw that under the surface he was miserable.

"It's a great nuisance," he said. "It'll be better when it's over."

"Wait a *min*ute! Perhaps pictures are in the wrong hands."

Brimmer, the Party Member, was announced, and going to meet him I slid over to the door on one of those gossamer throw rugs and practically into his arms.

He was a nice-looking man, this Brimmer – a little on the order of Spencer Tracy, but with a stronger face and a wider range of reactions written up in it. I couldn't help thinking, as he and Stahr smiled and shook hands and squared off, that they were two of the most alert men I had ever seen. They were very conscious of each other immediately – both as polite to me as you please, but with a softening of the ends of their sentences when they turned in my direction.

"What are you people trying to do?" demanded Stahr. "You've got my young men all upset."

"That keeps them awake, doesn't it?" said Brimmer.

"First we let half a dozen Russians study the plant," said Stahr. "As a model plant, you understand. And then you try to break up the unity that makes it a model plant."

"The unity?" Brimmer repeated. "Do you mean what's known as The Company Spirit?"

"Oh, not that," said Stahr, impatiently. "It seems to be *me* you're after. Last week a writer came into my office – a drunk – a man who's been floating around for years just two steps out of the bughouse – and began telling me my business."

Brimmer smiled.

"You don't look to me like a man who could be told his business, Mr Stahr."

They would both have tea. When I came back, Stahr was telling a story about the Warner Brothers and Brimmer was laughing with him.

"I'll tell you another one," Stahr said. "Balanchine the Russian dancer* had them mixed up with the Ritz Brothers.* He didn't know which ones he was training and which ones he was working for. He used to go around saying, 'I cannot train these Warner Brothers to dance.'"

It looked like a quiet afternoon. Brimmer asked him why the producers didn't back the anti-Nazi League.

"Because of you people," said Stahr. "It's your way of getting at the writers. In the long view you're wasting your time. Writers are children – even in normal times they can't keep their minds on their work."

"They're the farmers in this business," said Brimmer pleasantly. "They grow the grain but they're not in at the feast. Their feeling towards the producer is like the farmers' resentment of the city fellow."

I was wondering about Stahr's girl – whether it was all over between them. Later, when I heard the whole thing from Kathleen, standing in the rain in a wretched road called

Goldwyn Avenue, I figured out that this must have been a week after she sent him the telegram. She couldn't help the telegram. The man got off the train unexpectedly and walked her to the registry office without a flicker of doubt that this was what she wanted. It was eight in the morning, and Kathleen was in such a daze that she was chiefly concerned about how to get the telegram to Stahr. In theory you could stop and say, "Listen, I forgot to tell you, but I met a man." But this track had been laid down so thoroughly, with such confidence, such struggle, such relief, that when it came along, suddenly cutting across the other, she found herself on it like a car on a closed switch. He watched her write the telegram, looking directly at it across the table, and she hoped he couldn't read it upside down...

When my mind came back into the room, they had destroyed the poor writers – Brimmer had gone so far as to admit they were "unstable".

"They are not equipped for authority," said Stahr. "There is no substitute for will. Sometimes you have to fake will when you don't feel it at all."

"I've had that experience."

"You have to say, 'It's got to be like this – no other way' – even if you're not sure. A dozen times a week that happens to me. Situations where there is no real reason for anything. You pretend there is."

"All leaders have felt that," said Brimmer. "Labour leaders, and certainly military leaders."

"So I've had to take an attitude in this Guild matter. It looks to me like a try for power, and all I am going to give the writers is money."

"You give some of them very little money. Thirty dollars a week."

"Who gets that?" asked Stahr, surprised.

"The ones that are commodities and easy to replace."

"Not on my lot," said Stahr.

"Oh, yes," said Brimmer. "Two men in your shorts department get thirty dollars a week."

"Who?"

"Man named Ransome – man named O'Brien."

Stahr and I smiled together.

"Those are not writers," said Stahr. "Those are cousins of Cecilia's father."

"There are some in other studios," said Brimmer.

Stahr took his teaspoon and poured himself some medicine from a little bottle.

"What's a fink?" he asked suddenly.

"A fink? That's a strike-breaker or a company tec."

"I thought so," said Stahr. "I've got a fifteen-hundred-dollar writer that every time he walks through the commissary keeps saying 'Fink!' behind other writers' chairs. If he didn't scare hell out of them, it'd be funny."

Brimmer laughed.

"I'd like to see that," he said.

"You wouldn't like to spend a day with me over there?" suggested Stahr.

Brimmer laughed with genuine amusement.

"No, Mr Stahr. But I don't doubt but that I'd be impressed. I've heard you're one of the hardest-working and most efficient men in the entire West. It'd be a privilege to watch you, but I'm afraid I'll have to deny myself."

Stahr looked at me.

"I like your friend," he said. "He's crazy, but I like him." He looked closely at Brimmer: "Born on this side?"

"Oh, yes. Several generations."

"Many of them like you?"

"My father was a Baptist minister."

"I mean, are many of them Reds? I'd like to meet this big Jew that tried to blow over the Ford factory. What's his name—"

"Frankensteen?"*

"That's the man. I guess some of you believe in it."

"Quite a few," said Brimmer drily.

"Not you," said Stahr.

A shade of annoyance floated across Brimmer's face.

"Oh, yes," he said.

"Oh, no," said Stahr. "Maybe you did once."

Brimmer shrugged his shoulders.

"Perhaps the boot's on the other foot," he said. "At the bottom of your heart, Mr Stahr, you know I'm right."

"No," said Stahr, "I think it's a bunch of tripe."

"…you think to yourself, 'He's right,' but you think the system will last out your time."

"You don't really think you're going to overthrow the government."

"No, Mr Stahr. But we think perhaps you are."

They were nicking at each other – little pricking strokes like men do sometimes. Women do it, too, but it is a joined battle then with no quarter. But it is not pleasant to watch men do it, because you never know what's next. Certainly it wasn't improving the tonal associations of the room for me, and I moved them out the French window into our golden-yellow California garden.

It was midsummer, but fresh water from the gasping sprinklers made the lawn glitter like spring. I could see Brimmer look at it with a sigh in his glance – a way they have. He opened up big outside – inches taller than I thought and broad-shouldered. He reminded me a little of Superman when he takes off his spectacles. I thought he was as attractive as men can be who don't really care about women as such. We played a round-robin game of ping-pong, and he handled his bat well. I heard Father come into the house singing that damned 'Little Girl, You've Had a Busy Day', and then breaking off, as if he remembered we weren't speaking any more. It was half-past six – my car was standing in the drive, and I suggested we go down to the Trocadero for dinner.

Brimmer had that look that Father O'Ney had that time in New York when he turned his collar around and went with Father and me to the Russian Ballet. He hadn't quite ought to be here. When Bernie, the photographer, who was waiting there for some big game or other, came up to our table, he looked trapped – Stahr made Bernie go away, and I would like to have had the picture.

Then, to my astonishment, Stahr had three cocktails, one after the other.

"Now I know you've been disappointed in love," I said.

"What makes you think that, Cecilia?"

"Cocktails."

"Oh, I never drink, Cecilia. I get dyspepsia – I've never been tight."

I counted them: "…two – *three*."

"I didn't realize. I couldn't taste them. I thought there was something the matter."

A silly glassy look darted into his eye – then passed away.

"This is my first drink in a week," said Brimmer. "I did my drinking in the Navy."

The look was back in Stahr's eye – he winked fatuously at me and said:

"This soapbox son-of-a-bitch has been working on the Navy."

Brimmer didn't know quite how to take this. Evidently he decided to include it with the evening, for he smiled faintly, and I saw Stahr was smiling too. I was relieved when I saw it was safely in the great American tradition, and I tried to take hold of the conversation, but Stahr seemed suddenly all right.

"Here's my typical experience," he said very succinctly and clearly to Brimmer. "The best director in Hollywood – a man I never interfere with – has some streak in him that wants to slip a pansy into every picture, or something on that order. Something offensive. He stamps it in deep like a watermark so I can't get it out. Every time he does it the Legion of Decency* moves a step forward, and something has to be sacrificed out of some honest film."

"Typical organizational trouble," agreed Brimmer.

"Typical," said Stahr. "It's an endless battle. So now this director tells me it's all right because he's got a Directors' Guild and I can't oppress the poor. That's how you add to my troubles."

"It's a little remote from us," said Brimmer smiling. "I don't think we'd make much headway with the directors."

"The directors used to be my pals," said Stahr proudly.

It was like Edward VII's boast that he had moved in the best society in Europe.*

"But some of them have never forgiven me," he continued, "for bringing out stage directors when sound came in. It put them on their toes and made them learn their jobs all over, but they never did really forgive me. That time we imported a whole new hogshead full of writers, and I thought they were great fellows till they all went red."

Gary Cooper came in and sat down in a corner with a bunch of men who breathed whenever he did and looked as if they lived off him and weren't budging. A woman across the room looked around and turned out to be Carole Lombard* – I was glad that Brimmer was at least getting an eyeful.

Stahr ordered a whiskey-and-soda and, almost immediately, another. He ate nothing but a few spoonfuls of soup and he said all the awful things about everybody being lazy so-and-sos and none of it mattered to *him*, because he had lots of money – it was the kind of talk you heard whenever Father and his friends were together. I think Stahr realized that it sounded pretty ugly outside of the proper company – maybe he had never heard how it sounded before. Anyhow he shut up and drank off a cup of black coffee. I loved him, and what he said didn't change that, but I hated Brimmer to carry off this impression. I wanted him to see Stahr as a sort of technological virtuoso, and here Stahr had been playing the wicked overseer to a point he would have called trash if he had watched it on the screen.

"I'm a production man," he said, as if to modify his previous attitude. "I like writers – I think I understand them. I don't want to kick anybody out if they do their work."

"We don't want you to," said Brimmer pleasantly. "We'd like to take you over as a going concern."

Stahr nodded grimly.

"I'd like to put you in a roomful of my partners. They've all got a dozen reasons for having Fitts* run you fellows out of town."

"We appreciate your protection," said Brimmer with a certain irony. "Frankly we *do* find you difficult, Mr Stahr – precisely because you are a paternalistic employer and your influence is very great."

Stahr was only half-listening.

"I never thought," he said, "that I had more brains than a writer has. But I always thought that his brains *belonged* to me – because I knew how to use them. Like the Romans – I've heard that they never invented things but they knew what to do with them. Do you see? I don't say it's right. But it's the way I've always felt – since I was a boy."

This interested Brimmer – the first thing that had interested him for an hour.

"You know yourself very well, Mr Stahr," he said.

I think he wanted to get away. He had been curious to see what kind of man Stahr was, and now he thought he knew. Still hoping things would be different, I rashly urged him to ride home with us, but when Stahr stopped by the bar for another drink I knew I'd made a mistake.

It was a gentle, harmless, motionless evening with a lot of Saturday cars. Stahr's hand lay along the back of the seat touching my hair. Suddenly I wished it had been about ten years ago – I would have been nine. Brimmer about eighteen and working his way through some Midwestern college, and

Stahr twenty-five, just having inherited the world and full of confidence and joy. We would both have looked up to Stahr so, without question. And here we were in an adult conflict, to which there was no peaceable solution, complicated now with the exhaustion and drink.

We turned in at our drive, and I drove around to the garden again.

"I must go along now," said Brimmer. "I've got to meet some people."

"No, stay," said Stahr. "I never have said what I wanted. We'll play ping-pong and have another drink, and then we'll tear into each other."

Brimmer hesitated. Stahr turned on the floodlight and picked up his ping-pong bat, and I went into the house for some whiskey – I wouldn't have dared disobey him.

When I came back, they were not playing, but Stahr was batting a whole box of new balls across to Brimmer, who turned them aside. When I arrived, he quit and took the bottle and retired to a chair just out of the floodlight, watching in dark dangerous majesty. He was pale – he was so transparent that you could almost watch the alcohol mingle with the poison of his exhaustion.

"Time to relax on Saturday night," he said.

"You're not relaxing," I said.

He was carrying on a losing battle with his instinct towards schizophrenia.

"I'm going to beat up Brimmer," he announced after a moment. "I'm going to handle this thing personally."

"Can't you pay somebody to do it?" asked Brimmer.

I signalled him to keep quiet.

"I do my own dirty work," said Stahr. "I'm going to beat hell out of you and put you on a train."

He got up and came forward, and I put my arms around him, gripping him.

"Please *stop* this!" I said. "Oh, you're being so bad."

"This fellow has an influence over you," he said darkly. "Over all you young people. You don't know what you're doing."

"Please go home," I said to Brimmer.

Stahr's suit was made of slippery cloth, and suddenly he slipped away from me and went for Brimmer. Brimmer retreated backwards around the table. There was an odd expression in his face, and afterwards I thought it looked as if he were saying, "Is *this* all? This frail, half-sick person holding up the whole thing."

Then Stahr came close, his hands going up. It seemed to me that Brimmer held him off with his left arm a minute, and then I looked away – I couldn't bear to watch.

When I looked back, Stahr was out of sight below the level of the table, and Brimmer was looking down at him.

"Please go home," I said to Brimmer.

"All right." He stood looking down at Stahr as I came around the table. "I always wanted to hit ten million dollars, but I didn't know it would be like this."

Stahr lay motionless.

"Please go," I said.

"I'm sorry. Can I help—"

"No. Please go. I understand."

He looked again, a little awed at the depths of Stahr's repose, which he had created in a split second. Then he went quickly away over the grass, and I knelt down and shook Stahr. After a moment he came awake with a terrific convulsion and bounced up on his feet.

"Where is he?" he shouted.

"Who?" I asked innocently.

"That American. Why in hell did you have to marry him, you damn fool?"

"Monroe – he's gone. I didn't marry anybody."

I pushed him down in a chair.

"He's been gone half an hour," I lied.

The ping-pong balls lay around in the grass like a constellation of stars. I turned on a sprinkler and came back with a wet handkerchief, but there was no mark on Stahr – he must have been hit in the side of the head. He went off behind some trees and was sick, and I heard him kicking up some earth over it. After that he seemed all right, but he wouldn't go into the house till I got him some mouthwash, so I took back the whiskey bottle and got a mouthwash bottle. His wretched essay at getting drunk was over. I've been out with college freshmen, but for sheer ineptitude and absence of the Bacchic spirit it unquestionably took the cake. Every bad thing happened to him, but that was all.

* * *

We went in the house; the cook said Father and Mr Marcus and Fleishacker were on the veranda, so we stayed in the "processed-leather room". We both sat down in a couple of places and seemed to slide off, and finally I sat on a fur rug and Stahr on a footstool beside me.

"Did I hit him?" he asked.

"Oh, yes," I said. "Quite badly."

"I don't believe it." After a minute he added: "I didn't want to hurt him. I just wanted to chase him out. I guess he got scared and hit me."

If this was his interpretation of what had happened, it was all right with me.

"Do you hold it against him?"

"Oh, no," he said. "I was drunk." He looked around. "I've never been in here before – who did this room? Somebody from the studio?

"Well, I'll have to get out of here," he said in his old pleasant way. "How would you like to go out to Doug Fairbanks's ranch and spend the night?" he asked me. "I know he'd love to have you."

That's how the two weeks started that he and I went around together. It only took one of them for Louella to have us married.

[The manuscript ends at this point.]

Synopsis of Unwritten Chapters

Although Fitzgerald never completed his final novel before his death and the text reproduced in this volume probably amounts to two thirds (itself only a draft version) of the intended final story, the author left behind many working notes and letters indicating how *The Last Tycoon* would have continued. In addition to these indications, Edmund Wilson, the editor of the first edition of the novel (1941), benefited from the input of Sheilah Graham and Frances Kroll, Fitzgerald's lovers in his final years, in his efforts to put together a synopsis of the unwritten episodes. Wilson's research, as well as that of other scholars such as Matthew J. Bruccoli, the editor of the 1993 Cambridge University Press edition, have made it possible to outline the direction in which Fitzgerald intended to take the plot. It must be noted, however, that Fitzgerald had a habit of heavily revising and reshaping his novels as he wrote successive drafts, so the summary below should only be read as a speculative attempt at recreating Fitzgerald's plans at first-draft stage.

It would appear that, after the point at which the manuscript stops, Stahr was to have gone on a summer trip to the East Coast, ostensibly to talk to his company's stockholders about the labour disputes within the organization between the unions and executives. Another reason seems to have been the producer's desire to get to see Washington, and this presented Fitzgerald with the opportunity to contrast the glamour- and money-driven world of Hollywood with the civic ideals of the nation's founders – a thematic juxtaposition which, as Edmund Wilson points out, had already been introduced in the first chapter, when the Hollywood delegation tried to visit Andrew Jackson's Hermitage. It is unclear how Stahr's business talks go in Washington, but he falls seriously ill in the city due to the heat.

The central issue in the dispute that prompted the trip is a proposed general wage cut, over which there has been disagreement between Brady and Stahr. When the latter returns to Hollywood, he finds out that his partner has, behind his back, imposed a fifty-per-cent cut across the entire company, reneging on a promise that only the writers and executives would sacrifice part of their salary in order to spare the lower-paid employees. Stahr, who is generally opposed to unions but endeavours to be a generous and protective employer, is appalled by Brady's ruthlessness, and the two fall out acrimoniously. Stahr also quarrels with Wylie White, who feels that the former is responsible for the cut, but White finally manages to convince Stahr about the necessity of a company union.

Stahr becomes romantically involved with Cecilia, but it is made clear to her that he really loves Kathleen. When Cecilia relates this information to her father, he tries to blackmail Stahr. In response, Stahr decides to dump Cecilia and, during a heated confrontation, he counters Brady's threats with the revelation that he knows that Brady had in the past been involved in the murder of an ex-lover's husband. But Brady has another card up his sleeve in the form of W. Bronson Smith, the studio engineer and union man whom Kathleen has married. Brady cynically decides to side with the unions in their power struggle against

Stahr, while at the same time stoking Smith's jealousy and desire for revenge, and the two start plotting against Stahr. It is unclear whether Fitzgerald had in mind a murder plot, or a plan to trap Stahr in an adulterous situation so that Smith could sue. Whatever the nature of Brady and Smith's machinations, it appears that Stahr is saved by Pete Zavras, the camera man.

At this point Stahr's health is worsening, and he has stopped making films altogether. He has a final fling with Kathleen, but he cannot bring himself to commit to a relationship with her. Since he is afraid that Brady will succeed in having him murdered, he decides to use his partner's own methods against him, and plans to have Brady killed. The details of the plot are not known, but Stahr arranges to leave for New York while it is being carried out. At the airport he separately meets Kathleen and Cecilia one last time, and while he is airborne he has a change of heart and vows to call off the murder as soon as he has landed in New York; unfortunately the plane crashes, Stahr dies in the accident and Brady is murdered. Fitzgerald had started to write a scene in which three children find the wreckage of the plane and loot the dead passengers, before one of them finally tells a local judge about what they have found – but he may have decided against including it in his last plan for the novel.

The scene of Stahr's funeral was to highlight Hollywood's hypocrisy, describing how various industry figures are eager to be seen mourning, while, in Cecilia's imagination, Stahr's spirit shouts "Trash!" at them. Ironically, one of the pall-bearers, the actor Johnny Swanson, has been invited by mistake, but the fact that he is seen to have been so close to the dead producer gives his career a boost and he is inundated with offers of roles. Fitzgerald also foreshadows the lawyer Mort Fleishacker's imminent rise up the Hollywood ranks. It is also revealed that Cecilia, who has had an affair with Wylie White, has been badly affected by the deaths of her father and Stahr, and has developed tuberculosis; she has been narrating her story from a sanatorium. Fitzgerald was also thinking of including an epilogue in which Kathleen, who may by now have separated from W. Bronson Smith, is portrayed standing outside Stahr's former studio, highlighting her status as an outsider to the industry.

Note on the Text

The text in the present edition is based on the first edition of *The Last Tycoon* (1941), edited by Edmund Wilson. The Cambridge University Press edition of *The Love of the Last Tycoon*, edited by Matthew J. Bruccoli, has been consulted and some of Wilson's editorial emendations have been undone or modified accordingly. The spelling and punctuation have been anglicized, standardized, modernized and made consistent throughout.

Notes

p. 3, *Lolly Parsons's*: A reference to Louella Parsons (1880–1972), a famous Hollywood gossip columnist.

p. 6, *Tory*: Used to describe American loyalists to the British throne during the American War of Independence.

p. 6, *If the bonus army conquered Washington*: A reference to an unsuccessful march on Washington, DC, by thousands of First World War veterans demanding early payment of veterans' bonuses.

p. 10, *Guy Lombardo*: Guy Lombardo (1902–77) was the leader of the popular band the Royal Canadians.

p. 10, *'Top Hat' and 'Cheek to Cheek'*: Songs by Irving Berlin (1888–1989) for the musical film *Top Hat* (1935).

p. 10, *Andrew Jackson*: Andrew Jackson (1767–1845) was the seventh President of the United States. The Hermitage is the name of the house and plantation he owned in Nashville, Tennessee.

p. 11, *Laemmle*: Carl Laemmle (1867–1939) was one of the most important early American film producers and the founder of Universal Pictures.

p. 12, *Cortés or Balboa*: A reference to the Spanish conquistadors Hernán Cortés (1485–1547) and Vasco Núñez de Balboa (c.1475–1519)

p. 15, *Old Hickory... Spoils System*: Old Hickory was the popular nickname for Andrew Jackson (see third note to p. 10), who is erroneously referred to as America's tenth president here. New Orleans was the location of a famous battle against the British in 1815 led by Jackson, at that time an army general. As president, he dismantled the Second Bank of the United States and encouraged a patronage system which gave administrative posts to party loyalists.

p. 18, *'Lost'... 'Gone'*: 'Lost' (1936) is a song by Phil Ohman (1896–1954), Johnny Mercer (1909–76) and Macy O. Teetor. 'Gone' (1936) is a song composed by Franz Waxman (1906–67), with lyrics by Gus Kahn (1886–1941).

p. 21, *Charles Francis Adams*: Charles Francis Adams Jr (1835–1915), part of the Adams political dynasty, was a railway executive and historian. Wylie goes on to paraphrase famous comments he made in his autobiography, published in 1916.

p. 21, *Gould, Vanderbilt, Carnegie, Astor*: Examples of American business tycoons: Jay Gould (1836–92), Cornelius Vanderbilt (1843–99), Andrew Carnegie (1835–1919) and John Jacob Astor (1763–1848).

p. 23, *42nd Street*: A popular 1933 musical film directed by Lloyd Bacon and choreographed by Busby Berkeley.

p. 26, *all the kingdoms*: See Luke 4:15.

p. 27, *Tom Mix or Bill Hart*: Tom Mix (1880–1940) and William S. Hart (1864–1946) were stars of the early Westerns.

p. 27, *Come, come, I love you only*: From the song 'My Hero' by Stanislaus Stange (1862–1917) for his adaptation of the operetta *The Chocolate Soldier* (1909) by Oscar Straus (1870–1954).

p. 28, *Will Rogers... Hollywood's St Francis*: Will Rogers (1879–1935) was a hugely popular actor, entertainer and humourist, known for his good nature and moral lifestyle.

p. 33, *DeMille*: Cecil B. DeMille (1881–1959) was an important Hollywood director and producer, mostly remembered for his historical epics.

p. 35, *the Emperor and the Old Guard*: A reference to Napoleon Bonaparte (1769–1821) and the most high-ranking regiment of his imperial guards, made up of veterans.

p. 36, *Griffith*: D.W. Griffith (1875–1948) was one of the most important early film directors, whose 1915 masterpiece *The Birth of a Nation* pioneered many new techniques.

p. 38, *Morgan's*: Possibly a reference to the actor Frank Morgan (1890–1949).

p. 38, *Tout passe... éternité*: "Everything comes to an end. – Only robust art is eternal" (French), ll. 41–42 of the poem 'L'Art' (1858) by Théophile Gautier (1811–72).

p. 39, *the Prince of Denmark*: Introduced later in the text as "Prince Agge", who was a real historical figure: Prince Aage of Denmark (1887–1940) was a cousin of the King of Denmark who renounced his rights to the throne and joined the foreign legion. According to Fitzgerald's notes, he is visiting Stahr's company "to learn about pictures from the beginning".

p. 43, *Georgie Jessel*: George Jessel (1898–1981) was a famous entertainer, actor and producer.

p. 48, *Reinhardt's Miracle*: A play, based on a medieval legend, written by Karl Vollmöller (1878–1948) and directed by Max Reinhardt (1873–1943), which was restaged on Broadway in 1924, having premiered in London in 1911.

p. 50, *Margaret Sullavan*: Margaret Sullavan (1911–60) was a Hollywood actress who specialized in playing romantic leads.

p. 50, *Colman*: Ronald Colman (1891–1958) was an English actor who often played the role of the archetypal English gentleman in Hollywood productions.

p. 51, *a Eugene O'Neill play*: Eugene O'Neill (1888–1953) was an Irish American playwright who specialized in realist dramas featuring disillusioned, contemplative characters.

p. 51, *Carroll and McMurray*: A reference to the Hollywood actors Madeleine Carroll (1906–87) and Fred MacMurray (1907–91). These names were changed by Wilson to the fictitious "Corliss and McKelway", perhaps because of unfounded libel fears.

p. 52, *Hays*: A reference to Will H. Hays (1879–1954), the president of the Motion Picture Producers and Distributors of America, who in 1930 established a code regulating the content of movies.

p. 55, *Joe Breen*: Joseph Breen (1888–1965), a film censor for the Motion Picture Producers and Distributors of America.

p. 60, *Bernadotte*: The name of the current Swedish royal house, of French origin, which came to power in 1810. Prince Agge, being part of the Danish royal family, would not have been related to the Bernadottes.

p. 60, *Hell's Angels or Ben Hur*: *Hell's Angels* (1930) and *Ben Hur* (1925) were historical epics, directed by Howard Hughes (1905–76) and Fred Niblo (1874–1948) respectively, which went over their production budgets but met with major success at the box office.

p. 63, *Nicolay's biography*: A reference to *Abraham Lincoln: A History* by Lincoln's former secretaries John G. Nicolay (1832–1901) and John Hay (1838–1905), first published in 1890.

p. 66, *Knights of Columbus*: An American Catholic fraternal organization founded in Connecticut in 1882.

p. 69, *Claudette Colbert*: Claudette Colbert (1903–96) was a Hollywood actress often cast in romantic comedies.

p. 69, *coureur du bois*: More correctly known as *coureur des bois*, literally "runner of the woods" (French), a term used to designate French Canadian fur traders.

p. 71, *Cary*: The Hollywood star Cary Grant (1904–86).

p. 72, *Sidney Howard*: Sidney Howard (1891–1939), a Pulitzer Prize-winning screenwriter and playwright.

p. 73, *Tracy*: Spencer Tracy (1900–67), a major Hollywood actor.

p. 74, *Manon*: Presumably a film adaptation of the French novel *Manon Lescaut* (1731) by Abbé Prévost (1697–1763).

p. 79, *Aeschylus... Diogenes... Asclepius... Menander*: Aeschylus (525/24–456/55 BC) was the first of the great classical Athenian tragedians; Diogenes of Sinope (fourth century BC) was a Greek philosopher and founder of the Cynic school of thought; Asclepius was the god of medicine in Greek mythology; and Menander (*c.*342–*c.*292 BC) was the best-known dramatist of Athenian New Comedy. In the 1941 edition Edmund Wilson substituted "Euripides" for "Diogenes" and "Aristophanes" for "Asclepius", second-guessing Fitzgerald's intentions and believing he was correcting mistakes in the author's draft, but, as Matthew J. Bruccoli points out in the Cambridge University Press edition, there is no evidence to suggest Fitzgerald got confused in his intended references.

p. 89, *'The Thundering Beat of My Heart'*: A reference to 'The Beat of My Heart' (1934), a song composed by Harold Spina (1906–97), with lyrics by Johnny Burke (1908–64).

p. 90, *tapped for Bones*: Chosen for the elite Skull and Bones society at Yale University.

p. 90, *Benny Goodman playing 'Blue Heaven'*: Benny Goodman (1909–86) was a jazz clarinettist and band leader. 'My Blue Heaven' (1924) was a popular song composed by Walter Donaldson (1893–1947), with lyrics by George Whiting (1884–1943).

p. 90, *Paul Whiteman with 'When Day Is Done'*: Paul Whiteman (1890–1967) was a popular jazz band leader. 'When Day Is Done' (1926) is the English version, with lyrics by B.G. Desylva (1895–1950), of the German song 'Madonna' (1924) by Robert Katscher (1894–1942).

p. 90, *'Little Girl, You've Had a Busy Day'*: The original song is called 'Little Man, You've Had a Busy Day' (1934) and was composed by Mabel Wayne (1904–78), with lyrics by Maurice Sigler (1901–61) and Al Hoffman (1902–60).

p. 90, *'Lovely to Look at'*: A song composed by Jerome Kern (1885–1945), with lyrics by Dorothy Fields (1905–74) and Jimmy McHugh (1894–1969), for the musical film *Roberta* (1935).

p. 92, *They asked me how I knew... my true love was true*: The beginning of the song 'Smoke Gets in Your Eyes' (1933), composed by Jerome Kern (1885–1945), with lyrics by Otto Harbach (1873–1963).

p. 95, *Sonja Henie*: Sonja Henie (1912–69) was a Norwegian Olympic figure skater and Hollywood actress.

p. 100, *John Barrymore and Pola Negri*: John Barrymore (1882–1942) was an American stage and film actor. Pola Negri (1897–1987) was a Polish-born Hollywood actress.

p. 100, *Connie Talmadge*: Constance Talmadge (1898–1973) was a film actress of the silent era.

p. 102, *Glenn Miller playing 'I'm on a See-Saw'*: Glenn Miller (1904–44) was the leader of a popular swing band. 'I'm on a See-Saw' (1934) is a song composed by Vivian Ellis (1904–96), with lyrics by Desmond Carter (1895–1939).

p. 104, *Randolph Hearst*: William Randolph Hearst (1863–1951) was a US newspaper tycoon and politician.

p. 110, *McKinley*: William McKinley (1843–1901) was the twenty-fifth President of the United States.

p. 110, *John Gilbert*: John Gilbert (1899–1936) was a major actor of the silent era, specializing in romantic lead roles.

p. 110, *The Hairy Ape*: A 1922 play by Eugene O'Neill.

p. 120, *Spengler*: Oswald Spengler was a German historian and philosopher who is most famous for his *The Decline of the West* (1918).

p. 121, *Sir Francis Drake had nailed his plaque to the boulder on the shore*: The English explorer Sir Francis Drake (*c.*1540–96) reportedly left a brass plaque where he landed in northern California in 1579. A plaque which purported to be Drake's emerged in 1936, but it was subsequently proven to be a hoax.

p. 122, *Emerson*: Ralph Waldo Emerson (1803–82), writer and poet, leader of the Transcendentalist movement.

p. 122, *Rosicrucian*: Pertaining to the Rosicrucian Order, an esoteric society whose teachings are said to be based on secret teachings from antiquity.

p. 126, *La Borwitz... Fleishacker, etc.*: This list mixes fictitious and actual Hollywood figures. Jean Harlow (1911–37) was a Hollywood megastar and sex symbol whose life was cut tragically short. Douglas Fairbanks Sr (1883–1939) was a major actor, producer and director. Spyros Skouras (1893–1971) was an important Greek-born Hollywood executive. For Colman see second note to p. 50.

p. 131, *In disgrace with fortune and men's eyes*: From the first line of Shakespeare's Sonnet 29.

p. 132, *Buddy Ebsen... Harry Davenport... Donald Crisp*: Buddy Ebsen (1908–2003), Harry Davenport (1886–1949) and Donald Crisp (1880–1974) were well-established character actors in Hollywood at the time.

p. 134, *Sex Fifth Avenue*: A pun on Saks Fifth Avenue, the upmarket New York department store.

p. 139, *Gary Cooper*: Gary Cooper (1901–61) was a Hollywood actor well-known for his cowboy roles.

p. 139, *Lord Charnwood*: A reference to the 1916 biography *Abraham Lincoln* by the British writer and politician Godfrey Benson, 1st Baron Charnwood (1864–1945).

p. 148, *the Black-and-Tans*: Special constables recruited from Britain in 1920 to help the Royal Irish Constabulary fight the Republican insurgents.

p. 151, *Beautiful Doll*: Probably a reference to the song 'Oh, You Beautiful Doll' (1911), composed by Nat D. Ayer (1887–1952), with lyrics by A. Seymour Brown (1885–1947).

p. 154, *Harry Bridges*: Harry Bridges (1901–90) was a union leader in San Francisco who became the head of International Longshore and Warehouse Union.

p. 154, *The New Masses*: A left-wing magazine aligned with the Communist Party.

p. 154, *the "I AM" cult*: The name of an occultist Californian sect active in the 1930s.

p. 155, *Doctor Caligari and Salvador Dalí's Le Chien andalou*: *The Cabinet of Doctor Caligari* is a 1920 German Expressionist horror film directed by Robert Wiene (1873–1938); *Un chien andalou* is a 1929 surrealist short film directed by Luis Buñuel (1900–83), in collaboration with Salvador Dalí (1904–89).

p. 155, *Communist Manifesto*: The influential 1848 pamphlet by Karl Marx (1818–83) and Friedrich Engels (1820–95).

p. 156, *Fanny Brice*: Fanny Brice (1891–51) was a comedian, singer and actress who was most famous for her radio series *The Baby Snooks Show*.

p. 158, *Balanchine the Russian dancer*: George Balanchine (1904–83) was a Russian ballet dancer who moved to the US and worked in Hollywood.

p. 158, *the Ritz Brothers*: A 1930s and '40s comedy act formed by three brothers: Al (1901–65), Jimmy (1904–85) and Harry (1907–86).

p. 161, *Frankensteen*: Richard Frankensteen (1907–77) was a union official who was beaten, along with his colleague Walter Reuther (1907–70), by strike-breakers at the Ford plant in Detroit in 1937. He was not Jewish as Stahr seems to think.

p. 163, *Legion of Decency*: A Catholic organization formed in 1934 to curb indecency in movies.

p. 164, *Edward VII's boast… best society in Europe*: King Edward VII (1841–1910) was known for his fondness for fashion in high society, especially during the years he was still Prince of Wales, under the reign of his mother, Queen Victoria.

p. 164, *Carole Lombard*: Carole Lombard (1908–42) was a Hollywood actress who starred in many comedies.

p. 165, *Fitts*: Buron Fitts (1895–1973) was the District Attorney for Los Angeles County. He was rumoured to have close links with studio bosses.

Extra Material

on

F. Scott Fitzgerald's

The Last Tycoon

F. Scott Fitzgerald's Life

Early Life

Francis Scott Key Fitzgerald was born on 24th September 1896 at 481 Laurel Avenue in St Paul, Minnesota. Fitzgerald, who would always be known as "Scott", was named after Francis Scott Key, the author of 'The Star-Spangled Banner' and his father's second cousin three times removed. His mother, Mary "Mollie" McQuillan, was born in 1860 in one of St Paul's wealthier streets, and would come into a modest inheritance at the death of her father in 1877. His father, Edward Fitzgerald, was born in 1853 near Rockville, Maryland. A wicker-furniture manufacturer at the time of Fitzgerald's birth, his business would collapse in 1898 and he would then take to the road as a wholesale grocery salesman for Procter & Gamble. This change of job necessitated various moves of home and the family initially shifted east to Buffalo, New York, in 1898, and then on to Syracuse, New York, in 1901. By 1903 they were back in Buffalo and in March 1908 they were in St Paul again after Edward lost his job at Procter & Gamble. The *déclassé* Fitzgeralds would initially live with the McQuillans and then moved into a series of rented houses, settling down at 599 Summit Avenue.

Schooling and Early Writings

This itinerancy would disrupt Fitzgerald's early schooling, isolating him and making it difficult to make many friends at his various schools in Buffalo, Syracuse and St Paul. The first one at which Fitzgerald would settle for a prolonged period was the St Paul Academy, which he entered in September 1908. It was here that Fitzgerald would achieve his first appearance in print, 'The Mystery of the Raymond Mortgage', which appeared in the St Paul Academy school magazine *Now and Then* in October 1909. 'Reade, Substitute Right Half' and 'A Debt of Honor' would follow in the February and March 1910 numbers, and 'The Room with the Green Blinds' in the June 1911 number. His reading at this time was dominated by adventure stories and the other typical literary interests of a turn-of-the-century American teen, with the novels of G.A. Henty, Walter Scott's *Ivanhoe* and Jane Porter's *The Scottish Chiefs* among his favourites; their influence was apparent in the floridly melodramatic tone of his early pieces, though themes that would recur throughout Fitzgerald's mature fiction, such as the social difficulties of the outsider, would be introduced in these stories. An interest in the theatre also surfaced at this time, with Fitzgerald writing and taking the lead role in *The Girl from Lazy J*, a play that would be performed with a local amateur-dramatic group, the Elizabethan Drama Club, in August 1911. The group would also produce *The Captured Shadow* in 1912, *The Coward* in 1913 and *Assorted Spirits* in 1914.

At the end of the summer of 1911, Fitzgerald was once again uprooted (in response to poor academic achievements) and moved to the Newman School, a private Catholic school in Hackensack, New Jersey. He was singularly unpopular with the other boys, who considered him aloof and overbearing. This period as a social pariah at Newman was a defining time for Fitzgerald, one that would be echoed repeatedly in his fiction, most straightforwardly in the "Basil" stories, the most famous of which, 'The Freshest Boy', would appear in *The Saturday Evening Post* in July 1928 and is clearly autobiographical in its depiction of a boastful schoolboy's social exclusion.

Hackensack had, however, the advantage of proximity to New York City, and Fitzgerald began to get to know Manhattan, visiting a series of shows, including *The Quaker Girl* and *Little Boy Blue*. His first publication in Newman's school magazine, *The Newman News*, was 'Football', a poem written in an attempt to appease his peers following a traumatic incident on the football field that led to widespread accusation of cowardice, compounding the young writer's isolation. In his last year at Newman he would publish three stories in *The Newman News*.

Father Fay and the Catholic Influence   Also in that last academic year Fitzgerald would encounter the prominent Catholic priest Father Cyril Sigourney Webster Fay, a lasting and formative connection that would influence the author's character, oeuvre and career. Father Fay introduced Fitzgerald to such figures as Henry Adams and encouraged the young writer towards the aesthetic and moral understanding that underpins all of his work. In spite of the licence and debauchery for which Fitzgerald's life and work are often read, a strong moral sense informs all of his fiction – a sense that can be readily traced to Fay and the author's Catholic schooling at Newman. Fay would later appear in thinly disguised form as Amory Blaine's spiritual mentor, and man of the world, Monsignor Darcy, in *This Side of Paradise*.

Princeton   Fitzgerald's academic performance was little improved at Newman, and he would fail four courses in his two years there. In spite of this, in May 1913 Fitzgerald took the entrance exams for Princeton, the preferred destination for Catholic undergraduates in New Jersey. He would go up in September 1913, his fees paid for through a legacy left by his grandmother Louisa McQuillan, who had died in August.

At Princeton Fitzgerald would begin to work in earnest on the process of turning himself into an author: in his first year he met confrères and future collaborators John Peale Bishop and Edmund Wilson. During his freshman year Fitzgerald won a competition to write the book and lyrics for the 1914–15 Triangle Club (the Princeton dramatic society) production *Fie! Fie! Fi-Fi!* He would also co-author, with Wilson, the 1915–16 production, *The Evil Eye*, and the lyrics for *Safety First*, the 1916–17 offering. He also quickly began to contribute to the Princeton humour magazine *The Princeton Tiger*, while his reading tastes had moved on to the social concerns of George Bernard Shaw, Compton Mackenzie and H.G. Wells. His social progress at Princeton also seemed assured as Fitzgerald was approached by the Cottage Club (one of Princeton's exclusive eating clubs) and prominence in the Triangle Club seemed inevitable.

September 1914 and the beginning of Fitzgerald's sopho-more year would mark the great calamity of his Princeton education, causing a trauma that Fitzgerald would approach variously in his writing (notably in *This Side of Paradise* and Gatsby's abortive "Oxford" career in *The Great Gatsby*). Poor academic performance meant that Fitzgerald was barred from extra-curricular activities; he was therefore unable to perform in *Fie! Fie! Fi-Fi!*, and took to the road with the production in an attendant capacity. Fitzgerald's progress at the Triangle and Cottage clubs stagnated (he made Secretary at Triangle nonethe-less, but did not reach the heights he had imagined for himself), and his hopes of social dominance on campus were dashed.

The second half of the 1914–15 academic year saw a brief *Ginevra King* improvement and subsequent slipping of Fitzgerald's performance *and Ill Health* in classes, perhaps in response to a budding romance with Ginevra King, a sixteen-year-old socialite from Lake Forest, Illinois. Their courtship would continue until January 1917. King would become the model for a series of Fitzgerald's characters, including Judy Jones in the 1922 short story 'Winter Dreams', Isabelle Borgé in *This Side of Paradise* and, most famously, Daisy Miller in *The Great Gatsby*. In November 1915 Fitzgerald's academic career was once again held up when he was diagnosed with malaria (though it is likely that this was in fact the first appearance of the tuberculosis that would sporadically disrupt his health for the rest of his life) and left Princeton for the rest of the semester to recuperate. At the same time as all of this disruption, however, Fitzgerald was building a head of steam in terms of his literary production. Publications during this period included stories, reviews and poems for Princeton's *Nassau Literary Magazine*.

The USA entered the Great War in May 1917 and a week later *Army* Fitzgerald joined up, at least partly motivated by the fact that his *Commission*

185

uncompleted courses at Princeton would automatically receive credits as he signed up. Three weeks of intensive training and the infantry commission exam soon followed, though a commission itself did not immediately materialize. Through the summer he stayed in St Paul, undertaking important readings in William James, Henri Bergson and others, and in the autumn he returned to Princeton (though not to study) and took lodgings with John Biggs Jr, the editor of the *Tiger*. More contributions appeared in both the *Nassau Literary Magazine* and the *Tiger*, but the commission finally came and in November Fitzgerald was off to Fort Leavenworth, Kansas, where he was to report as a second lieutenant in the infantry. Convinced that he would die in the war, Fitzgerald began intense work on his first novel, *The Romantic Egoist*, the first draft of which would be finished while on leave from Kansas in February 1918. The publishing house Charles Scribner's Sons, despite offering an encouraging appreciation of the novel, rejected successive drafts in August and October 1918.

Zelda Sayre   As his military training progressed and the army readied Fitzgerald and his men for the fighting in Europe, he was relocated, first to Camp Gordon in Georgia, and then on to Camp Sheridan, near Montgomery, Alabama. There, at a dance at the Montgomery Country Club in July, he met Zelda Sayre, a beautiful eighteen-year-old socialite and daughter of a justice of the Alabama Supreme Court. An intense courtship began and Fitzgerald soon proposed marriage, though Zelda was nervous about marrying a man with so few apparent prospects.

As the armistice that ended the Great War was signed on 11th November 1918, Fitzgerald was waiting to embark for Europe, and had already been issued with his overseas uniform. The closeness by which he avoided action in the Great War stayed with Fitzgerald, and gave him another trope for his fiction, with many of his characters, Amory Blaine from *This Side of Paradise* and Jay Gatsby among them, attributed with abortive or ambiguous military careers. Father Fay, who had been involved, and had tried to involve Fitzgerald, in a series of mysterious intelligence operations during the war, died in January 1919, leaving Fitzgerald without a moral guide just as he entered the world free from the restrictions of Princeton and the army. Fay would be the dedicatee of *This Side of Paradise*.

Literary   Fitzgerald's first move after the war was to secure gainful
Endeavours employment at Barron Collier, an advertising agency, producing copy for trolley-car advertisements. At night he continued to work hard at his fiction, collecting 112 rejection slips over this period. Relief was close at hand, however, with *The Smart Set* printing a revised version of 'Babes in the Wood' (a short story that had previous appeared in *Nassau Literary Magazine* and

that would soon be cannibalized for *This Side of Paradise*) in their September 1919 issue. *The Smart Set*, edited by this time by H.L. Mencken and George Jean Nathan, who would both become firm supporters of Fitzgerald's talent, was a respected literary magazine, but not a high payer; Fitzgerald received $30 for this first appearance. Buoyed by this, and frustrated by his job, Fitzgerald elected to leave work and New York and return to his parents' house in St Paul, where he would make a concerted effort to finish his novel. As none of the early drafts of *The Romantic Egoist* survive, it is impossible to say with complete certainty how much of that project was preserved in the draft of *This Side of Paradise* that emerged at St Paul. It was, at any rate, more attractive to Scribner in its new form, and the editor Maxwell Perkins, who would come to act as both editor and personal banker for Fitzgerald, wrote on 16th September to say that the novel had been accepted. Soon after he would hire Harold Ober to act as his agent, an arrangement that would continue throughout the greatest years of Fitzgerald's output and that would benefit the author greatly, despite sometimes causing Ober a great deal of difficulty and anxiety. Though Fitzgerald would consider his novels the artistically important part of his work, it would be his short stories, administered by Ober, which would provide the bulk of his income. Throughout his career a regular supply of short stories appeared between his novels, a supply that became more essential and more difficult to maintain as the author grew older.

Newly confident after the acceptance of *This Side of Paradise*, *Success* Fitzgerald set about revising a series of his previous stories, securing another four publications in *The Smart Set*, one in *Scribner's Magazine* and one in *The Saturday Evening Post*, an organ that would prove to be one of the author's most dependable sources of income for many years to come. By the end of 1919 Fitzgerald had made $879 from writing: not yet a living, but a start. His receipts would quickly increase. Thanks to Ober's skilful assistance *The Saturday Evening Post* had taken another six stories by February 1920, at $400 each. In March *This Side of Paradise* was published and proved to be a surprising success, selling 3,000 in its first three days and making instant celebrities of Fitzgerald and Zelda, who would marry the author on 3rd April, her earlier concerns about her suitor's solvency apparently eased by his sudden literary success. During the whirl of 1920, the couple's *annus mirabilis*, other miraculous portents of a future of plenty included the sale of a story, 'Head and Shoulders', to Metro Films for $2,500, the sale of four stories to *Metropolitan Magazine* for $900 each and the rapid appearance of *Flappers and Philosophers*, a volume of stories, published by

Scribner in September. By the end of the year Fitzgerald, still in his mid-twenties, had moved into an apartment on New York's West 59th Street and was hard at work on his second novel.

Zelda discovered she was pregnant in February 1921, and in May the couple headed to Europe where they visited various heroes and attractions, including John Galsworthy. They returned in July to St Paul, where a daughter, Scottie, was born on 26th October. Fitzgerald was working consistently and well at this time, producing a prodigious amount of high-quality material. *The Beautiful and Damned*, his second novel, was soon ready and began to appear as a serialization in *Metropolitan Magazine* from September. Its publication in book form would have to wait until March 1922, at which point it received mixed reviews, though Scribner managed to sell 40,000 copies of it in its first year of publication. Once again it would be followed within a few months by a short-story collection, *Tales of the Jazz Age*, which contained such classics of twentieth-century American literature as 'May Day', 'The Diamond as Big as the Ritz' and 'The Curious Case of Benjamin Button'.

1923 saw continued successes and a first failure. Receipts were growing rapidly: the Hearst organization bought first option in Fitzgerald's stories for $1,500, he sold the film rights for *This Side of Paradise* for $10,000 and he began selling stories to *The Saturday Evening Post* for $1,250 each. *The Vegetable*, on the other hand, a play that he had been working on for some time, opened in Atlantic City and closed almost immediately following poor reviews, losing Fitzgerald money. By the end of the year his income had shot up to $28,759.78, but he had spent more than that on the play and fast living, and found himself in debt as a result.

The Fitzgeralds' high living was coming at an even higher price. In an attempt to finish his new project Fitzgerald set out for Europe with Zelda and landed up on the French Riviera, a situation that provided the author with the space and time to make some real progress on his novel. While there, however, Zelda met Édouard Jozan, a French pilot, and began a romantic entanglement that put a heavy strain on her marriage. This scenario has been read by some as influencing the final drafting of *The Great Gatsby*, notably Gatsby's disillusionment with Daisy. It would also provide one of the central threads of *Tender Is the Night*, while Gerald and Sara Murphy, two friends they made on the Riviera, would be models for that novel's central characters. Throughout 1924 their relations became more difficult, their volatility was expressed through increasingly erratic behaviour and by the end of the year Fitzgerald's drinking was developing into alcoholism.

Some progress was made on the novel, however, and a draft was sent to Scribner in October. A period of extensive and crucial revisions followed through January and February 1925, with the novel already at the galley-proof stage. After extensive negotiations with Max Perkins, the new novel also received its final title at about this time. Previous titles had included *Trimalchio* and *Trimalchio in West Egg*, both of which Scribner found too obscure for a mass readership, despite Fitzgerald's preference for them, while *Gold-Hatted Gatsby*, *On the Road to West Egg*, *The High-Bouncing Lover* and *Among Ash Heaps and Millionaires* were also suggestions. Shortly before the novel was due to be published, Fitzgerald telegrammed Scribner with the possible title *Under the Red, White and Blue*, but it was too late, and the work was published as *The Great Gatsby* on 10th April. The reception for the new work was impressive, and it quickly garnered some of Fitzgerald's most enthusiastic reviews, but its sales did not reach the best-seller levels the author and Scribner had hoped for.

Fitzgerald was keen to get on with his work and, rather mis- *Paris* guidedly, set off to Paris with Zelda to begin his next novel. Paris at the heart of the Roaring Twenties was not a locale conducive to careful concentration, and little progress was made on the new project. There was much socializing, however, and Fitzgerald invested quite a lot of his time in cementing his reputation as one of the more prominent drunks of American letters. The couple's time was spent mostly with the American expatriate community, and among those he got to know there were Edith Wharton, Gertrude Stein, Robert McAlmon and Sylvia Beach of Shakespeare & Company. Perhaps the most significant relationship with another writer from this period was with Ernest Hemingway, with whom Fitzgerald spent much time (sparking jealousy in Zelda), and for whom he would become an important early supporter, helping to encourage Scribner to publish *The Torrents of Spring* and *The Sun Also Rises*, for which he also gave extensive editorial advice. The summer of 1925 was again spent on the Riviera, but this time with a rowdier crowd (which included John Dos Passos, Archibald MacLeish and Rudolph Valentino) and little progress was made on the new book. February 1926 saw publication of the inevitable follow-up short-story collection, this time *All the Sad Young Men*, of which the most significant pieces were 'The Rich Boy', 'Winter Dreams' and 'Absolution'. All three are closely associated with *The Great Gatsby*, and can be read as alternative routes into the Gatsby story.

With the new novel still effectively stalled, Fitzgerald decamped *Hollywood* to Hollywood at the beginning of 1927, where he was engaged by United Artists to write a flapper comedy that was never produced in the end. These false starts were not, however, adversely affecting Fitzgerald's earnings, and 1927 would represent the highest annual earnings the author had achieved so far: $29,757.87, largely from short-story sales. While in California Fitzgerald began a dalliance with Lois Moran, a seventeen-year-old aspiring actress – putting further strain on his relationship with Zelda. After the couple moved back east (to Delaware) Zelda began taking ballet lessons in an attempt to carve a niche for herself that might offer her a role beyond that of the wife of a famous author. She would also make various attempts to become an author in her own right. The lessons would continue under the tutelage of Lubov Egorova when the Fitzgeralds moved to Paris in the summer of 1928, with Zelda's obsessive commitment to dance practice worrying those around her and offering the signs of the mental illness that was soon to envelop her.

Looking for a steady income stream (in spite of very high earnings expenditure was still outstripping them), Fitzgerald set to work on the "Basil" stories in 1928, earning $31,500 for nine that appeared in *The Saturday Evening Post*, forcing novel-writing into the background. The next year his *Post* fee would rise to $4,000 a story. Throughout the next few years he would move between the USA and Europe, desperate to resuscitate that project, but make little inroads.

Zelda's Mental   By 1930 Zelda's behaviour was becoming more and more
Illness   erratic, and on 23rd April she was checked into the Malmaison clinic near Paris for rest and assistance with her mental problems. Deeply obsessed with her dancing lessons, and infatuated with Egorova, she discharged herself from the clinic on 11th May and attempted suicide a few days later. After this she was admitted to the care of Dr Oscar Forel in Switzerland, who diagnosed her as schizophrenic. Such care was expensive and placed a new financial strain on Fitzgerald, who responded by selling another series of stories to the *Post* and earning $32,000 for the year. The most significant story of this period was 'Babylon Revisited'. Zelda improved and moved back to Montgomery, Alabama, and the care of the Sayre family in September 1931. That autumn Fitzgerald would make another abortive attempt to break into Hollywood screenwriting.

At the beginning of 1932 Zelda suffered a relapse during a trip to Florida and was admitted to the Henry Phipps Psychiatric Clinic in Baltimore. While there she would finish work on a novel, *Save Me the Waltz*, that covered some of the same material her husband was using in his novel about the Riviera. Upon completion she sent the manuscript to Perkins at Scribner, without passing it to her husband, which caused much distress. Fitzgerald helped her to edit the book nonetheless, removing much of the material he intended to use, and Scribner accepted it and published it on 7th October. It received poor reviews and did not sell. Finally accepting that she had missed her chance to become a professional dancer, Zelda now poured her energies into painting. Fitzgerald would organize a show of these in New York in 1934, and a play, *Scandalabra*, that would be performed by the Junior Vagabonds, an amateur Baltimore drama group, in the spring of 1933.

His own health now beginning to fail, Fitzgerald returned *Final Novel* to his own novel and rewrote extensively through 1933, finally submitting it in October. *Tender Is the Night* would appear in serialized form in *Scribner's Magazine* from January to April 1934 and would then be published, in amended form, on 12th April. It was generally received positively and sold well, though again not to the blockbusting extent that Fitzgerald had hoped for. This would be Fitzgerald's final completed novel. He was thirty-seven.

With the receipts for *Tender Is the Night* lower than had *Financial* been hoped for and Zelda still erratic and requiring expensive *Problems and* medical supervision, Fitzgerald's finances were tight. From this *Artistic Decline* point on he found it increasingly difficult to produce the kind of high-quality, extended pieces that could earn thousands of dollars in glossies like *The Saturday Evening Post*. From 1934 many of his stories were shorter and brought less money, while some of them were simply sub-standard. Of the outlets for this new kind of work, *Esquire* proved the most reliable, though it only paid $250 a piece, a large drop from his salad days at the *Post*.

March 1935 saw the publication of *Taps at Reveille*, another collection of short stories from Scribner. It was a patchy collection, but included the important 'Babylon Revisited', while 'Crazy Sunday' saw his first sustained attempt at writing about Hollywood, a prediction of the tendency of much of his work to come. His next significant writing came, however, with three articles that appeared in the February, March and April 1936 numbers of *Esquire*: 'The Crack-up', 'Pasting It Together' and 'Handle with Care'. These essays were brutally confessional, and irritated many of those around Fitzgerald, who felt that he was airing his dirty laundry in public. His agent Harold Ober was concerned that by publicizing his own battles with depression and alcoholism he would give the high-paying glossies the impression that he was unreliable, making future magazine work harder to come by. The pieces have, however, come to be regarded as Fitzgerald's greatest non-fiction work and are an essential document in both the construction of his own legend and in the mythologizing of the Jazz Age.

Later in 1936, on the author's fortieth birthday in September, *Suicide* he gave an interview in *The New York Post* to Michael Mok. *Attempt and* The article was a sensationalist hatchet job entitled 'Scott *Worsening* Fitzgerald, 40, Engulfed in Despair' and showed him as a *Health* depressed dipsomaniac. The publication of the article wounded Fitzgerald further and he tried to take his own life through an overdose of morphine. After this his health continued to deteriorate and various spates in institutions followed, for influenza, for tuberculosis and, repeatedly, in attempts to treat his alcoholism.

His inability to rely on his own physical and literary powers meant a significant drop in his earning capabilities; by 1937 his debts exceeded $40,000, much of which was owed to his agent Ober and his editor Perkins, while Fitzgerald still had to pay Zelda's medical fees and support his daughter and himself. A solution to this desperate situation appeared in July: MGM would hire him as a screenwriter at $1,000 a week for six months. He went west, hired an apartment and set about his work. He contributed to various films, usually in collaboration with other writers, a system that irked him. Among these were *A Yank at Oxford* and various stillborn projects, including *Infidelity*, which was to have starred Joan Crawford, and an adaptation of 'Babylon Revisited'. He only received one screen credit from this time, for an adaptation of Erich Maria Remarque's novel *Three Comrades*, produced by Joseph Mankiewicz. His work on this picture led to a renewal of his contract, but no more credits followed.

Sheila Graham　　While in Hollywood Fitzgerald met Sheila Graham, a twenty-eight-year-old English gossip columnist, with whom he began an affair. Graham, who initially attracted Fitzgerald because of her physical similarity to the youthful Zelda, became Fitzgerald's partner during the last years of his life, cohabiting with the author quite openly in Los Angeles. It seems unlikely that Zelda, still in medical care, ever knew about her. Graham had risen up from a rather murky background in England and Fitzgerald set about improving her with his "College of One", aiming to introduce her to his favoured writers and thinkers. She would be the model for Kathleen Moore in *The Last Tycoon*.

Among the film projects he worked on at this time were *Madame Curie* and *Gone with the Wind*, neither of which earned him a credit. The contract with MGM was terminated in 1939 and Fitzgerald became a freelance screenwriter. While engaged on the screenplay for *Winter Carnival* for United Artists, Fitzgerald went on a drinking spree at Dartmouth College, resulting in his getting fired. A final period of alcoholic excess followed, marring a trip to Cuba with Zelda in April and worsening his financial straits. At this time Ober finally pulled the plug and refused to lend Fitzgerald any more money, though he would continue to support Scottie, Fitzgerald's daughter, whom the Obers had effectively brought up. The writer, now his own agent, began working on a Hollywood novel based on the life of the famous Hollywood producer Irving Thalberg.

Hollywood would also be the theme of the last fiction Fitzgerald would see published; the Pat Hobby stories. These appeared in *Esquire* beginning in January 1940 and continued till after the author's death, ending in July 1941 and appearing in each monthly number between those dates.

In November 1940 Fitzgerald suffered a heart attack and was told to rest, which he did at Graham's apartment. On 21st December he had another heart attack and died, aged just forty-four. Permission was refused to bury him in St Mary's Church in Rockville, Maryland, where his father had been buried, because Fitzgerald was not a practising Catholic. Instead he was buried at Rockville Union Cemetery on 27th December 1940. In 1975 Scottie Fitzgerald would successfully petition to have her mother and father moved to the family plot at St Mary's. *Death*

Following Fitzgerald's death his old college friend Edmund Wilson would edit Fitzgerald's incomplete final novel, shaping his drafts and notes into *The Last Tycoon*, which was published in 1941 by Scribner. Wilson also collected Fitzgerald's confessional *Esquire* pieces and published them with a selection of related short stories and essays as *The Crack-up and Other Pieces and Stories* in 1945.

Zelda lived on until 1948, in and out of mental hospitals. After reading *The Last Tycoon* she began work on *Caesar's Things*, a novel that was not finished when the Highland hospital caught fire and she died, locked in her room in preparation for electro-shock therapy.

F. Scott Fitzgerald's Works

Fitzgerald's first novel, *This Side of Paradise*, set the tone for his later classic works. The novel was published in 1920 and was a remarkable success, impressing critics and readers alike. Amory Blaine, the directionless and guilelessly dissolute protagonist, is an artistically semi-engaged innocent, and perilously, though charmingly unconsciously, déclassé. His long drift towards destruction (and implicit reincarnation as Fitzgerald himself) sees Blaine's various arrogances challenged one by one as he moves from a well-heeled life in the Midwest through private school and middling social successes at Princeton towards a life of vague and unrewarding artistic involvement. Beneath Fitzgerald's precise observations of American high society in the late 1910s can be witnessed the creation of a wholly new American type, and Blaine would become a somewhat seedy role model for his generation. Fast-living and nihilist tendencies would become the character traits of Fitzgerald's set and the *This Side of Paradise*

Lost Generation more generally. Indeed, by the novel's end, it has become clear that Blaine's experiences of lost love, a hostile society and the deaths of his mother and friends have imparted important life lessons upon him. Blaine, having returned to a Princeton that he has outgrown and poised before an unknowable future, ends the novel with his Jazz Age *cogito*: "'I know myself,' he cried, 'but that is all.'"

Flappers and Philosophers   Fitzgerald's next publication would continue this disquisition on his era and peers: *Flappers and Philosophers* (1920) is a collection of short stories, including such famous pieces as 'Bernice Bobs Her Hair' and 'The Ice Palace'. The first of these tells the tale of Bernice, who visits her cousin Marjorie only to find herself rejected for being a stop on Marjorie's social activities. Realizing that she can't rid herself of Bernice, Marjorie decides to coach her to become a young femme fatale like herself – and Bernice is quickly a hit with the town boys. Too much of a hit though, and Marjorie takes her revenge by persuading Bernice that it would be to her social advantage to bob her hair. It turns out not to be and Bernice leaves the town embarrassed, but not before cutting off Marjorie's pigtails in her sleep and taking them with her to the station.

The Beautiful and Damned   *The Beautiful and Damned* (1922) would follow, another novel that featured a thinly disguised portrait of Fitzgerald in the figure of the main character, Anthony Patch. He was joined by a fictionalized version of Fitzgerald's new wife Zelda, whom the author married as *This Side of Paradise* went to press. The couple are here depicted on a rapidly downward course that both mirrored and predicted the Fitzgeralds' own trajectory. Patch is the heir apparent of his reforming grandfather's sizable fortune but lives a life of dissolution in the city, promising that he'll find gainful employment. He marries Gloria Gilbert, a great but turbulent beauty, and they gradually descend into alcoholism, wasting what little capital Anthony has on high living and escapades. When his grandfather walks in on a scene of debauchery, Anthony is disinherited and the Patches' decline quickens. When the grandfather dies, Anthony embarks on a legal case to reclaim the money from the good causes to which it has been donated and wins their case, although not before Anthony has lost his mind and Gloria her beauty.

Tales of the Jazz Age   Another volume of short stories, *Tales of the Jazz Age*, was published later in the same year, in accordance with Scribner's policy of quickly following successful novels with moneymaking collections of short stories. Throughout this period Fitzgerald was gaining for himself a reputation as America's premier short-story writer, producing fiction for a selection of high-profile "glossy" magazines and earning unparalleled fees for his efforts. The opportunities and the pressures of this commercial work, coupled with Fitzgerald's continued profligacy, led to a certain unevenness in his short fiction. This unevenness is clearly present in *Tales of the Jazz Age*, with some of Fitzgerald's very best work appearing beside some more average pieces. Among the great works are 'The Diamond as Big as the Ritz', the story of a family that live in seclusion on top of a mountain made of solid diamond and have their house guests routinely executed to keep their wealth secret, and the novella 'May Day', which offers a panorama of Manhattan's post-war social order as the anti-communist May Day Riots of 1919 unfold.

In spite of the apparent success that Fitzgerald was experiencing by this time, his next novel came with greater difficulty than his first four volumes. *The Great Gatsby* is the story of Jay Gatsby, born poor as James Gatz, an *arriviste* of mysterious origins who sets himself up in high style on Long Island's north shore only to find disappointment and his demise there. Like Fitzgerald, and some of his other characters, including Anthony Patch, Gatsby falls in love during the war, this time with Daisy Miller. Following Gatsby's departure, however, Daisy marries the greatly wealthy Tom Buchanan, which convinces Gatsby that he lost her only because of his penuriousness. Following this, Gatsby builds himself a fortune comparable to Buchanan's through mysterious and proscribed means and, five years after Daisy broke off their relations, uses his new-found wealth to throw a series of parties from an enormous house across the water from Buchanan's Long Island pile. His intention is to impress his near neighbour Daisy with the lavishness of his entertainments, but he miscalculates and the "old money" Buchanans stay away, not attracted by Gatsby's *parvenu* antics. Instead Gatsby approaches Nick Carraway, the novel's narrator (who took that role in one of the masterstrokes of the late stages of the novel's revision), Daisy's cousin and Gatsby's neighbour. Daisy is initially affected by Gatsby's devotion, to the extent that she agrees to leave Buchanan, but once Buchanan reveals Gatsby's criminal source of income she has second thoughts. Daisy, shocked by this revelation, accidentally kills Buchanan's mistress Myrtle in a hit-and-run accident with Gatsby in the car and returns to Buchanan, leaving Gatsby waiting for her answer. Buchanan then lets Myrtle's husband believe that Gatsby was driving the car and the husband shoots him, leaving him floating in the unused swimming pool of his great estate.

Of *All the Sad Young Men* (1926) the most interesting pieces are 'The Rich Boy', 'Winter Dreams' and 'Absolution'. All three

The Great Gatsby

All the Sad Young Men

195

have much in common with *The Great Gatsby*, with 'Winter Dreams' telling the tale of Dexter Green and Judy Jones, similar characters to Jay Gatsby and Daisy Miller. Much like Gatsby, Green raises himself from nothing with the intention of winning Jones's affections. And, like Gatsby, he finds the past lost. 'Absolution' is a rejected false start on *The Great Gatsby* and deals with a young boy's difficulties around the confessional and an encounter with a deranged priest.

'Babylon Revisited' is probably the greatest and most read story of the apparently fallow period between *The Great Gatsby* and *Tender Is the Night*. It deals with Charlie Wales, an American businessman who enacts some of Fitzgerald's guilt for his apparent abandonment of his daughter Scottie and wife Zelda. Wales returns to a Paris unknown to him since he gave up drinking. There he fights his dead wife's family for custody of his daughter, only to find that friends from his past undo his careful efforts.

Tender Is the Night   The next, and last completed, novel came even harder, and it would not be until 1934 that *Tender Is the Night* would appear. This novel was met by mixed reviews and low, but not disastrous sales. It has remained controversial among readers of Fitzgerald and is hailed by some as his masterpiece and others as an aesthetic failure. The plotting is less finely wrought than the far leaner *The Great Gatsby*, and apparent chronological inconsistencies and longueurs have put off some readers. The unremitting detail of Dick Diver's descent, however, is unmatched in Fitzgerald's oeuvre.

It begins with an impressive set-piece description of life on the Riviera during the summer of 1925. There Rosemary Hoyt, modelled on the real-life actress Lois Moran, meets Dick and Nicole Driver, and becomes infatuated with Dick. It is then revealed that Dick had been a successful psychiatrist and had met Nicole when she was his patient, being treated in the aftermath of being raped by her father. Now Dick is finding it difficult to maintain his research interests in the social whirl that Nicole's money has thrust him into. Dick is forced out of a Swiss clinic for his unreliability and incipient alcoholism. Later Dick consummates his relationship with Rosemary on a trip to Rome, and gets beaten by police after drunkenly involving himself in a fight. When the Divers return to the Riviera Dick drinks more and Nicole leaves him for Tommy Barban, a French-American mercenary soldier (based on Zelda's Riviera beau Édouard Jozan). Dick returns to America, where he becomes a provincial doctor and disappears.

Pat Hobby Stories   The "Pat Hobby" stories are the most remarkable product of Fitzgerald's time in Hollywood to see publication during the author's lifetime. Seventeen stories appeared in all, in consecutive issues of *Esquire* through 1940 and 1941. Hobby is a squalid Hollywood hack fallen upon hard times and with the days of his great success, measured by on-screen credits, some years behind him. He is a generally unsympathetic character and most of the stories depict him in unflattering situations, saving his own skin at the expense of those around him. It speaks to the hardiness of Fitzgerald's talent that even at this late stage he was able to make a character as amoral as Hobby vivid and engaging on the page. The Hobby stories are all short, evidencing Fitzgerald's skill in his later career at compressing storylines that would previously have been extrapolated far further.

Fitzgerald's final project was *The Last Tycoon*, a work which, in the partial and provisional version that was published after the author's death, has all the hallmarks of a quite remarkable work. He had begun writing it in 1939, while he was struggling to make a living as a Hollywood screenwriter. As he could not convince Scribner to pay him a full advance, he had to interrupt work on the novel constantly to devote his energies to other commissions. The aim was to write a novel that would be short and not get bogged down in complications as *Tender Is the Night* had, and that would deal with the inner workings of Hollywood – a subject matter which had not really been hitherto explored in fiction. More specifically, it would be inspired by the life of the producer Irving Thalberg, the "Boy Wonder" of Hollywood, and his fractious relationship with his partner at MGM studios Louis B. Mayer – a story which contains the typical Fitzgerald themes of aspiration and downfall.

Upon his death, the author left behind around 44,000 words of disjointed narrative, as well as various working notes and plans which indicate the direction the story would have taken. Sheilah Graham sent the material to the Scribner editor Maxwell Perkins, and the literary critic Edmund Wilson – a friend of Fitzgerald's from Princeton – volunteered to edit the material. It was published in 1941 under the title *The Last Tycoon: A Romance*, although Fitzgerald had not settled on a title (*Stahr: A Romance* and *The Love of the Last Tycoon: A Western* were among the ones he had considered).

The written portion of the novel, which it seems likely would have been rewritten extensively before publication (in accordance with Fitzgerald's previous practice), is a classic conjuring of the golden age of Hollywood through an ambiguous and suspenseful story of love and money. It is told from the point of view of Cecilia Brady, the daughter of the producer Bradogue, although the narration at times slips into omniscient third person. The first chapter sees Cecilia and other motion-picture insiders on an

The Last Tycoon

aeroplane that has to make an emergency landing in Nashville, Tennessee. She strikes up a conversation with Wylie White and Mr Schwartz. They plan to visit the Hermitage, the historic home of Andrew Jackson, but it is closed when they get there. She then bumps into the novel's protagonist Monroe Stahr, the Hollywood producer and younger business partner of her father's, and we are given a decription of the man and early indications of Cecilia's amorous feelings towards him. The plane takes off again after Stahr has lectured the pilot. In the next chapter the action jumps forward to an evening in July, when Cecilia visits Stahr and Brady's studios on the day of her father's birthday. There is an earthquake in which no one is injured, but the water mains have burst in the back lot of the studios. When he comes to inspect the flooding, he is transfixed by a female visitor who looks exactly like his deceased wife Minna, floating on a prop of a head of Shiva. Chapters 3 and 4 recount Stahr's next working day, during which, among other things, he learns that the camera man Pete Zavras has broken an arm in a suicide attempt, and he has to cancel the production of a film. He arranges a meeting with the woman whom he thought was Minna's lookalike, but it turns out that she is the unknown woman's friend Edna. Edna introduces him to Kathleen Moore, the stranger Stahr had been looking for, and the two decide to meet again at a dance. The following afternoon Stahr takes Kathleen to a house he owns by the sea, and they have a fling, but she leaves him a note saying she cannot be his, later revealing that she has just got married. Cecilia discovers her father having an affair with a co-worker in the studios, and Chapter 6 sees stars in informal talks with the union boss Brimmer. The manuscript ends with Stahr offering to spend a weekend together with Cecilia.

The notes that follow the completed portion of *The Last Tycoon* suggest that the story would have developed in a much more melodramatic direction, with Stahr embarking on transcontinental business trips, losing his edge, ordering murders and dying in an aeroplane crash (see the synopsis in this volume on pp. 170–73). If the rewrites around *Tender Is the Night* are anything to go by, it seems likely that Fitzgerald would have toned down Stahr's adventures before finishing the story: in the earlier novel, stories of matricide and other violent moments had survived a number of early drafts, only to be cut before the book took its final form.

– Richard Parker

Select Bibliography

Standard Edition:
The Cambridge University Press edition (1993) of *The Love of the Last Tycoon*, edited by Matthew J. Bruccoli, with extensive annotations, variants and background material, is the most authoritative edition to date.

Biographies:
Bruccoli, Matthew J., *Some Sort of Epic Grandeur: The Life of F. Scott Fitzgerald*, 2nd edn. (Columbia, SC: University of South Carolina Press, 2002)
Mizener, Arthur, *The Far Side of Paradise: A Biography of F. Scott Fitzgerald*, (Boston, MS: Houghton Mifflin, 1951)
Turnbull, Andrew, *Scott Fitzgerald* (Harmondsworth: Penguin, 1970)

Additional Recommended Background Material:
Curnutt, Kirk, ed., *A Historical Guide to F. Scott Fitzgerald* (Oxford: Oxford University Press, 2004)
Prigozy, Ruth, ed., *The Cambridge Companion to F. Scott Fitzgerald* (Cambridge: Cambridge University Press, 2002)

LATEST TITLES PUBLISHED BY **ALMA CLASSICS**

To order any of our titles and for up-to-date information about our current and forthcoming publications, please visit our website at:

www.almaclassics.com